Also by Catherine Forde

Fat Boy Swim
Skarrs
Think Me Back
The Finding

WOODMILL HIGH SCHOOL

CATHERINE FORDE

EGMONT

To Cally,
For your white magic

EGMONT
We bring stories to life

First published in Great Britain 2005
by Egmont Books Ltd
239 Kensington High Street
London W8 6SA

ISBN 1 4052 2176 3

1 3 5 7 9 10 8 6 4 2

A CIP catalogue record for this title is available from the British Library

Typeset by Avon DataSet Ltd, Bidford on Avon B50 4JH
Printed and bound in Great Britain by the CPI Group

'Witchcraft was overwhelmingly concerned with the individual, the local and the mundane.'

Edward J Conway & Lizanne Henderson,
from their essay 'Survival of Scottish witch belief'
in *The Scottish witch-hunt in context* ed. Julian Goodare,
Manchester University Press, 2002.

AUTHOR'S NOTE

I am indebted to the composer James Macmillan, who gave me permission to describe and dissect *The Confession of Isobel Gowdie* without knowing what Nicky Nevin and her classmates would have to say about it when they heard it.

Thanks, Jimmy!

I am also indebted to Alan, a real ranger in Mugdock Country Park, who walked me through history on a cold, icy morning.

CONTENTS

1

WHERE IT ENDED

So.

It *did* end up here:

Merlock Country Park on Hallowe'en night.

According to Isabella there was even supposed to be a full moon.

'Imagine. A witch's moon for us, Nicky. Perfect, eh?' Isabella hissed in my ear while we scrambled a low dyke, sneaking into the park.

To tell the truth, all I could see in the wet sky were clouds.

Not perfect; it's nuts, I thought, slithering all the way down a mud bank on my bum. Graceful as ever. Best jeans sodden before we'd even started. With no return bus to the city this late, I didn't know how the heck we were even making it home after we'd done what we'd come to do tonight. Hadn't factored that into The Plan.

Idiot, I grumbled to myself through slicing rain as I

aimed for the four silhouettes waiting below me on the pathway: Big Janet Pike, even bigger Margaret Muir, flanking Isabella like bodyguards. Wee Lizzie Brownie standing apart.

As ever, the randomer, the sadcase . . .

'Ten minutes' walk,' Isabella promised us, 'and we reach Gallow Hill.'

'*Whoooooo,*' either Janet or Margaret hooted. Sarky as per. Then both of them sniggered.

Not me.

I gulped.

Just wanted to go home. Turn back, up the mud slope, over the dyke. Then trudge seven miles of unlit country road all the way to Mum. Luke. Didn't care how wet or cold I got. How long it took. How beeling Mum (and Dad, if he came home on the late, late train from Aberdeen) would be. Even how pathetic I'd feel when Luke roasted me for what I'd already done to his precious Lizzie. I just wanted to wipe out everything that had led me to this place.

And start all over again.

But I couldn't, could I? Things had come too far. I'd made

sure of that. Now I was stuck in a moment and couldn't get out of it, as one of Luke's favourite song goes. Isabella would *never* let me quit. And anyway, as Luke would say, I was under her spell.

'All right, troops?' Isabella tutted after we'd bumped against and stumbled over each other in the pitch dark for five minutes. 'Torches on now. Nosy park rangers won't see us from here.'

'You sure, Bella?' Janet piped up. She was ahead of me.

'Pikey, I'm *always* sure,' Isabella snapped, her hand double-skelping Janet's face. Back. Forth. Sharp. Sting. In a reflex I winced while I rummaged in my backpack among ropes and candles for Luke's camping torch.

'Move it, Nevin,' Isabella growled at me. The sight of her face appearing in a burst of orange torchlight had me covering my eyes with my free hand and reeling backwards.

'Oops. Careful, Nicky,' Lizzie Brownie said, when I trod on her foot. That surprising voice of hers sang so close to my ear that I shivered.

Oops yourself! a wheedly voice mocked in my own

head as I shrugged Lizzie's steadying hand. You're the one wanting to be careful, missy, I sneered silently. But even as I bitched the words, in my heart I knew I was being rotten, rotten, rotten . . .

Lizzie'd been ultra-chuffed to be invited along tonight.

Sorry we've been mean.
Let's start again on Hallowe'en

the invitation I gave her said. Even the rhyme was my idea. Spent ages designing it on Luke's laptop, wishing I could have asked him to help me improve it. No chance under the circumstances, of course. Still, I was pleased with the final result: a card covered in dancing pumpkins and cute little witchies.

'Girls' night,' I'd told Lizzie, kid-on casual at the end of school. 'Gonna scare ourselves mental at Merlock Park.'

'Fine,' Lizzie had said, though she turned my invite over and over in her hands like she was waiting for some hidden message to appear. 'What's the occasion, Nicky?'

'Just Hallowe'en,' I'd shrugged, glad Lizzie was studying the card and not my face. 'We're bringing food.

Wine. Sleepover at mine after. It'll be a laugh . . .'

Liar.

With Mum sick like she was, no one ever, *ever* stayed over at mine any more. No. Once Isabella, Janet, Margaret and I'd taken care of business up Merlock we'd be heading back to party at Isabella's.

Minus Lizzie, of course.

How *she* got home after tonight, *if* she got home tonight . . . Well, that was her problem.

Something else I hadn't factored into The Plan . . .

All that mattered for now was luring Lizzie Brownie up Merlock Park.

So far, so good.

'It's darker out here with these torches *on*,' I chittered to her before I could stop myself. The pair of us had fallen into step together behind the sweep of my torch-beam, trailing the others enough to lose sight of them on a turn in the path ahead. Which meant they must have reached the base of Gallow Hill already. As blackness swallowed their lights I nearly stopped walking. Nearly said to Lizzie, 'Look. Let's just leave.'

Before something's done that can't be undone.

Honest. Believe me. Even at this, the eleventh hour and fifty-five minutes, I nearly cut out. Put a stop to what happened next. Except . . .

Well, I happened to flash Luke's torch in Lizzie's face before I opened my mouth and saved her. She hadn't spoken since we started walking and for one stomach-lurching second I feared the crunching of footsteps alongside my own was a trick: had Lizzie already scrammed? Had she scented danger with that sixth sense I'd convinced the others she must have. (What would be worse? Realising that Lizzie really *had* flown off, or having to admit to Isabella that I'd lost her before we did what we were here for?) You could say I was almost grateful to see Lizzie sticking by my side after all, even if the profile glowing in my pool of torchlight freaked me doolally.

See, I caught her unawares. She wasn't just *walking* beside me, peering through the downpour from the hood of her sour-smelling kagoule. Oh, no. Loopy Loner Lizzie's face was thrown back, her baldy buff-fluff excuse for hair exposed. Beneath that fading scratch scoring her forehead like a frown (*my* doing, as you'll learn if you can bear to hear me out) her eyes were closed, mouth open like she was talking away to herself. Soundlessly. Honest to God, I nearly lost it.

Lizzie Brownie looked *every* bit the weirdo *witch* we were out to prove she was tonight.

We're doing the right thing, I decided, calling ahead to the others, 'Wait for me!'

The pathway narrowed on the snake up to Gallow Hill. Trees closed around us, their roots catching our feet, their leaf-slimed branches clawing our faces. I'd to unconvince myself they were trying to restrain us – *Don't do this, girls. It's wrong* – and ignore the way even the rain's voice seemed to change as it hit their leaves. It hardened to blatter out a warning: *STOP. Don't go any further.* Big Margaret obviously caught the same vibe.

'Don't like this place, Nicky,' she whispered, lurching into a pothole on her bad ankle and clutching my arm.

'You're not here to like it, are you, stupid?'

Don't ask me how Isabella could have heard us talking, what with the rain rattling and the wind whistling out of tune to make the branches dance. Soon as Margaret spoke, however, Isabella swung her light into

Margaret's face, whipping the skirts of her ankle-length black mac after her. I'm not kidding, in that get-up she made a perfect stunt-double for the Wicked Stepmother in Snow White: cascading dark hair, glittering eyes, red lips. Beautiful. Cruel. She even blooming cackled like her, 'We've made it! Hallowe'en at the Drowning Pond. Let's drink to that.'

Isabella's fingers snapped an order for Janet to produce the fizzy plonk Isabella had made her lug in her backpack.

'*Saluti!*' Twisting open the screwtop lid, Isabella drank first, long and greedily, careless of the wine streaming down her chin.

'Who's next?' she asked, eyes swivelling from me to Margaret.

'I'll pass,' I said. Though I could fair have gone a swig of Dutch courage, even the sight of that wine made me gag.

In Isabella's restaurant we'd swallied pints of the sickly stuff while we planned and planned what was *finally* happening.

'Give Lizzie the bottle,' I said.

'Not before me –' snorted Margaret, grabbing the wine.

'And I'm after Mags.' Behind Lizzie's back Janet made

a pantomime of scratching at her scalp. Apelike.

'Dunno what bugs she's got tonight,' she muttered.

'Laid*eez*. Civil,' Isabella trilled daintily, although she tugged so hard when she pulled the wine from Margaret's mouth I heard glass click off enamel.

'Here, Lizzie,' Isabella said, wiping the bottle-neck clean with a flourish of her own black velvet scarf. The plonk must have gone straight to her head because she gave Lizzie a burst of song. I think it was meant to sound reggae.

'*Red, red wine –*,' she warbled into her ever-present imaginary mike – without irony, by the way – at Lizzie's face. '*You drink as much as you like.* We'll get on . . .'

A few more steps and we'd reached journey's end: the top of Gallow Hill. Clear of the trees now, we stood on a wooden bridge. It bisected the stretch of water lying at the hill's summit.

It was still pouring, cold rain driving into our faces, tap-dancing on our waterproofs. But underfoot, beneath the slimy planks of the bridge the rain plunged gently, hitting black water like a secret hushed. I could see its surface bubbling with tiny rain breaths when I skimmed it with the light of my torch.

Here was the Drowning Pond.

No wonder I was sweating ice beneath Luke's Goretex.

'Oi! Candles, Nevin. Move it!' Isabella bumped me with the full force of her hip, knocking my propped chin from my hands so I bit my tongue hard. Through the tears that sprang to my eyes, I could see two distorted Lizzies draining the dregs of Isabella's rotten wine.

'What are the candles for, Nicky?' she hiccupped.

'Hallowe'en spirit,' Isabella piped up, glaring me silent before I muddled an answer. She was rummaging in my backpack, paying out the rope I'd brought.

'And why that rope?'

'Hallowe'en game, Lizzie.'

Isabella wasn't singing now. Her voice was grim. Holding the torch beneath her chin she glanced quickly from me to Janet. *Are we ready?* The rope jiggled impatiently in her hand.

'What game? You're not tying someone up?'

I heard it: that first catch of fear in Lizzie's voice. *I'm not here to be part of your girls' night, am I?* Anxiety squeaked the soles of her tatty plimsolls, panicking them away from us along the wet bridge. As she flailed about in appeal to Janet, to me – *What's going on*? – I stepped forward, mouth open.

'Isabella –' I began, though I couldn't think what to say next. So I said nothing. Didn't intercede: *This is wrong. This is evil.* And – God forgive me – I didn't try to save Lizzie Brownie. I just looked to Isabella della Rosa, and I danced to her tune.

'*I'll* tell you why we're here, Lizzie,' Isabella was saying, her nod to Janet the signal for Lizzie's arms to be racked up her back exactly as they'd rehearsed on me.

'We're gonna dook. But not for apples this Hallowe'en. We're dooking a *strega*.'

Oh, believe me, we'd planned this next bit. Every detail. We knew the routine by heart.

The gagging. The binding.

Once Isabella decided we were going through with the ritual she had me scan copies from a library book I'd borrowed showing ancient illustrations of the way everything would have been done.

'Jan, once I gag Lizzie with my scarf you bend her over so Nicky and Mags can get her hands tied to her feet. Remember they've to cross in front of her. Then we chuck her in.'

Swimming the Witch they used to call it.

And right here, *right here* in Merlock Park was where they used to do it. They'd throw girls suspected of witchcraft into the water.

Waiting to see if they'd drown.

If they did – oops-a-daisy – that meant they were innocent.

Dead. But innocent.

However, if they floated to the surface . . .

Well, that meant the water, a symbol of Christian baptism, was rejecting them. So they were witches. The Devil's own. Fit to be dragged from the Drowning Pond, strangled till they were too near death to curse their accusers.

Then burned alive on Gallow Hill.

Strangling and burning? If it's any consolation, that wasn't in The Plan. Isabella couldn't see past swimming Lizzie Brownie. She'd latched on to that single idea. *What a blast, Nicky!* Obsessed. Same as she'd latched on to me when she realised I was Luke Nevin's sister. But that's going back too far . . .

We had Lizzie down, big Janet digging her goalie's knees into Lizzie's side, one hand forcing her head against the bridge while Margaret heeled off Lizzie's plimsolls, clawed down her socks.

'Man, her feet honk like rat's farts.'

'Just tie her, Mags. Thumbs to toes. Tight as you can,' Isabella instructed. She was setting black candles on the bridge, wafting a taper over them while Margaret and I did the dirty work. We grappled with Lizzie's ankles and wrists. For all she was shilpit, Lizzie bucked beneath us, and every time she struggled, her head scudded off the wooden struts of the bridge. Desperate.

I couldn't look at her face because I knew she was trying to say my name through the thick scarf bridling her mouth. Instead I bent low over her hands and feet, Luke's hood hiding me as my fingers worked at knotting the climbing rope I'd nicked from his room.

'Tighter,' rasped Isabella. 'Don't let witchy escape.'

'No chance, Bella.' Margaret was rolling Lizzie to feed the last rope around her waist, a double loop. 'She's trussed like a bubbly-jock.'

'Listen to her, cursing away.' Big Janet knelt beside Margaret, cocking her ear to Lizzie's gagged mouth. To see them both being so *brutal* with Lizzie you'd never believe me if I told you they were seriously lukewarm about doing any of this till tonight. Now though, now we were here in Merlock Park, you'd think they'd planned their actions in advance: the pair of them crossing themselves. Sl-o-w-l-y. Then shooting their arms out. Pushing at Lizzie to make her rock from side to side on her back.

'Hush-a-bye, witchy, on the hilltop . . .'

'Time all your evil came to a stop . . .'

they crooned, singing into Lizzie's eyes. Guffawing at each other. Looking to Isabella for approval. I couldn't share their laughter. Not when I could hear these frantic grunts from Lizzie that Isabella was aping as she joined Margaret and Janet on her knees. Grasping the rope that tethered Lizzie's hands to her feet, Isabella rocked her harder, more violently than before.

'Seasick, *strega*?' she sneered.

'Well, she's greetin' anyway,' chimed Margaret.

'Boo-hoo.' That was Janet.

'Can you blame her?' My own voice was a quaver. But it stopped Isabella.

'Cold feet, Nevin?'

She rose, yanking Lizzie towards me with one hand. The other scooped a candle from the bridge. She held it up between us. 'Fancy swapping places?'

When I gave no reply Isabella leaned in to me.

'You're in this *big time,* Nevin,' she reminded me. 'All your idea. Remember?'

Then Isabella drew the candle close to her face, one finger pointing to the livid, cratered skin of her forehead. 'You said we'd to punish Lizzie for doing *this,*' whispered Isabella, mouth downturned, 'and stealing Luke –'

'– *and* making me ill,' burped Janet, shuffling to kneel at one side of Isabella. '*And* hexing Mags at netball.'

Margaret, who had joined them, looked up at Isabella, tugging on her raincoat.

'Too right. I'd have played netball for Scotland if my ankle wasn't gubbed. Let's do this.'

We dragged Lizzie to the end of the bridge. I held the rope, but I didn't pull. I swear it. Does that make me any less guilty? After all, I was there, slithering, grabbing hold of the bridge, of big Janet, of Isabella's long coat, to stop myself joining Lizzie in the Drowning Pond.

Can't remember who gave the final shove. Honest. We were all skittering over each other, shoes filling with water, pond mud sucking at my feet, when I realised the bundle on the ground was gone. At my last sight of it,

Isabella was rolling it down the bank with her leg.

'*Ciao strega,*' she was singsonging, her outstretched arms embracing the night.

Then I didn't see any more.

Because on the bridge, all the candles guttered at once, and a huge screech of wind whipped the air.

2

NITS

Isabella was right: I *was* in this big time.

In fact, I started it.

Early September. Just into the new school year.

I clocked something crawling across the new girl's scalp. So I informed Isabella. Thought I was being ultra witty.

'Keep away from Lousy, there. She's got visitors.'

It was a horrible, mean thing to do. Should have kept my gob shut. Should have done the decent thing and had a private word with the school nurse. But I was just at the point where I'd have done *anything* to keep in with Isabella now that Luke was finished with her. *Anything.* Even so, even as I was cupping my hand to Isabella's ear, I sensed I'd triggered something *bad*.

I tried to backtrack, smacking my hand over my lips, mouthing, 'I'm rotten, me.' But the damage was done. Isabella della Rosa was impressed with me, and her seed of loathing for Lizzie Brownie was sown. Believe me, she would never, *ever* have noticed a zero like Lizzie otherwise.

It didn't help that this all happened during Personal and Social Development, our girls-only skive class where 'any sensitive issue in your complex adolescence', as the school handbook put it, was up for group discussion. Normally, in PSD, no one cheeped for forty-five minutes, and not just because it was timetabled first thing on a Monday. Truth is, there was no *way* us complex adolescents were prepared to group-discuss periods, hormones or sexual feelings with anyone. Hello? It was heinous enough having old goat Miss Groat from Biology presiding. A poker-faced hag like that wouldn't have known a sexual feeling if it licked her ass.

Even more off-putting than Old Groat, though, was having Isabella, Janet and Margaret in 4C. No matter how matey I'd grown with that trio over the summer, I knew fine that their ears were on 24/7 standby, pricked up and primed to broadcast the least smear of gynecological goss nationwide. Better by far to zip it in PSD. Accept the ever-increasing bushel of lines Groat doled out when the bell rang as routine homework.

It was the lesser of two evils.

Which is why no one seemed more surprised than

Miss Groat when Isabella, sullen at best throughout PSD, shot up her hand and hissed, 'Missss, Misssss, Missssss.' She was straining out of her seat like you'd do when you were bursting to pee your pants in baby class:

'Misss, Missss, Misssss. *Pleeeze,* Miss.'

This happened milliseconds after I'd noticed Lizzie Brownie's infestation and spread the word to Isabella. It was practically a miracle that I'd got away with whispering anything to anyone without Old Groat hearing and subjecting me to one of her verbal acid attacks, but she'd her back to the class. Affronted that not one groomed and deodorised girl in our class could volunteer a single idea on the subject of

GOOD PERSONAL HYGIENE,

she was brainstorming solo on the blackboard. She'd two columns going:

PROBLEM on the left *SOLUTION* on the right.

'Copy,' she snarled without looking over her shoulder, chalk running away with itself.

'Lucky Old Groat can write from experience,' I muttered to Isabella, pinching my nose, and plucking imaginary chin whiskers. This won me a huge smile. And, I noticed, an exchange of glares between my used-to-be chums, Yvonne and Caroline. They sat at the next table, the seat they'd been keeping for me since term began untaken.

Bad breath: *Clean teeth. Visit dentist.*

Body odour: *Bath/shower, use deodorant.*

Foot odour: *Bathe frequently, change socks, avoid synthetic footwear.*

Miss Groat was writing.

'*Madre de Dio*! Are we retards?' Isabella hissed at her tweedy back. In exasperation she threw her hair over her shoulder and started to write. I shrugged in agreement, scribbling down the next problem on Miss Groat's list.

Oily hair:

And I winced, a flush creeping my face when I wrote *o-i-l-y* as if the letters were leaving greasy fingerprints on my jotter. Maybe it was just me, but skanky hair came top of my major no-no list, worse than whiffy pits or custard-coated teeth. And I knew why. And I'd better come clean. Slight grease problem myself. Nothing major, and nothing *anyone* apart from Caroline and Yvonne – who were far too decent to grass me up – knew about. Naturally, I went overboard to ensure I was squeaky clean in the tresses department. Twice a day lathering my scalp till it tingled.

Still, I was super-sensitive to the condition of other people's hair, always checking up, the same way you're always checking up in the hope that someone's bum looks bigger than your own.

Or is it just me who does these things?

Anyway, there I was conducting my usual survey:

Did Yvonne's blonde bob look lanker than mine felt?

Was brainbox Elaine McCartney having problems with the old shoulder snow?

As per usual, every girl's hair looked uber-normal, no one's more so than Isabella. Her hair, like the rest of her beauty, depressed me. It was gorgeous. So long, that when she didn't wear it coiled in a thick black rope, she could sit on it. I practically heard it taunting me with its vitality as I scanned past the two pairs of ceramic-iron sleek, honey-streak curtains that framed Janet and Margaret's faces till I came to the end of our row.

There sat the new girl.

The one who'd moved into that foster home in Einstein Elaine McCartney's road.

Elizabeth Brownie.

I only knew her name because Old Groat had snapped it three times at regie before Lizzie answered, though that was the first time I'd ever paid any attention to her. If someone asked me to describe her before that PSD lesson I couldn't have. A blank she was in my mind's eye. A void. A nothing. Yet she'd been in 4C since term began and when I clocked the state of Lizzie that day, I didn't know how I could have missed her before.

For starters her hair minged worse than mine did when I'd flu last Christmas and left it unwashed for a week. It was matted and tuggy, straggling over her shoulders like rebellious straw. *Totally, actually, hideous,* as Isabella would say.

Then I noticed Lizzie Brownie was digging into her haystack with the point of her pencil; in and out, in and out of the same patch of thatch behind her ear. Lizzie was scratching away at herself so hard I could *hear* the scrape of lead against her scalp. Shuddering, yet unable to tear my eyes away – someone does something scumoid, you watch, yeah? Or is that just me again? – I felt my eyes widen as, still working away at the first location, thumb hooked round the pencil, Lizzie expanded her scratch-zone. Spreading out her hand she began to claw into her head with sweeping rotations of her fingers.

Five fingers, by the way.

My stomach lurched. There was one extra digit there. It branched, stunted and rubbery, from the side of Lizzie's left pinkie. Freakoid! Gross! Totally actually hideous.

That's what I was turning to show Isabella, when I realised, to cap it all, Lizzie's hair was *moving*.

'Miss. Miss. *Signorina*. Her head's crawling.'

Before Old Groat could demand, 'What is going on, ladies?' 4C was in uproar. With both arms cradling her hair, Isabella was on her feet, moving her desk as far away from Lizzie as she could.

'Keep her away,' she howled.

What wrong? What's up? Why are we moving? Sleepy Monday voices puzzled beneath the scrape and clatter and drag of wooden legs on lino.

Who? Nits? What? Where?

By the time Miss Groat had silenced the chaos with a whip-skite of Yvonne's ruler off the radiator, the biology room was transformed. A chasm yawned between Lizzie Brownie on one side of the class and everyone else.

'What is the meaning of this?' Old Groat blasted the cower of us. Huddling in a far corner of the room every last girl, including Yvonne and Caroline, was playing *Isabella says* and protecting her hair with her hands.

'Miss, she's mingin'.' Isabella's accusing finger pointed across the room.

At Lizzie Brownie.

Who was staring ahead of herself, perhaps even contemplating Miss Groat's final interrupted brainstorm brainwave: Cleanliness is next to Godline— I noticed that Lizzie's shoulders were drawn up and tense. She was chewing her bottom lip.

'Miss, she's lousy. Nicky Nevin saw.' Isabella nodded to me for backup, the gesture making her huge gold earrings wink: *Go on. Join in.*

'Miss. You can see them moving, Miss,' I began, and then I heard myself add, as the earrings flashed encouragement, 'It's disgustin'.'

Well. Everyone was with me on that: *Too right.* Here was 4C's first pro-active PSD group discussion. Of course we were all scratching away, raking through our own heads. Even hours after Lizzie Brownie had been sent home from school.

You do, don't you? You try not to, but can't help it. Just the idea of creepy crawly parasites running amok, taking up residency on *your* body, sets your skin dancing . . .

'It's auto-suggestion, stupid. Mind over matter. Dead easy to get the brain to trigger physical responses,' Luke explained later that night. Because Dad was working off-shore and, of course, Mum's hands couldn't manage it, he was landed the enviable job of picking through my hair with the special nit comb I'd had the mortification of having to buy because Mum couldn't do that for me either. The letter from school advised us all to examine our heads carefully following the discovery of a serious headlice infestation in a Fourth Year pupil.

Totally actually hideous!

'But you don't have cooties, Nick. Just fleas,' Luke reassured me, using the end of the comb to reproach me with a big-brotherly bop on the head. 'Couldn't *believe* the OTT state of you girlies squealing at each other. Especially Isabella.' Luke camped it up round Mum's chair to demonstrate, clapping his hands to his cheeks and flopping his wrists. '"*Omigod, omigod, omigod . . .*"'

'That new girl had *lice*,' I interrupted Luke before he went so Graham Norton that he started singing 'YMCA'! 'It was rank. She could have infected us all –'

'You're *not* infected, Nick. *A*ffected more like! Bet the girl with the nits was mortified. Hope you lot didn't give her a hard time.'

'Course we didn't,' I lied. 'She gets to skive school for a week thanks to me.' I wasn't looking at Luke. I was making myself busy rinsing my comb, checking the teeth, just in case.

I didn't mention that Isabella had hurled, 'Keep away from us, right?' at Lizzie Brownie while Miss Groat nipped into the class next door to ask Poofter Page to keep an eye on us so she could take Lizzie to the medical room.

Or that Margaret and Janet had chorused, 'Yeah, keep away . . .'

'. . . or you're getting it!'

Or that I'd sneered, 'Lousy Lizzie,' and the whole of

4C, apart from Yvonne and Caroline who were looking at me as if my head was on upside down, took up the chant.

Lousy Lizzie, Lousy Lizzie . . .

And that Lizzie had turned back and looked at us all. One by one. You could barely see her face through all that hair, but the expression on it was sullen like the sky before a downpour. She'd mouthed something.

You'll be sorry, I thought she'd said.

Lousy Lizzie.

That kind of nickname sticks. Like mud.

I knew I was doing something wrong, even as the insult was spilling out. Should have gulped, swallowed my cruelty, tasting how bad it must have felt for Lizzie, who had to skulk out of 4C with her head bowed.

See, I started it. It was all my fault . . .

3

ISABELLA

SUN SIGN: LEO ♌

RULING PLANET: SUN ☉

Leos typically have beautiful hair which they expect to be admired.

Leos can be cold-hearted and fickle when it comes to friendship . . .

Madre de Dio, one crumb of a compliment chucked at Nevin for spicing up Groatsy's garbage PSD, and you wanna have seen her wee chubby face.

All I said was '*Magnifico, cara mia!*' and blew her a kiss, and Nevin sprouted this beamer like I'd handed her an Oscar for World's Coolest Mate. Swollen with pride she was. Honest, I was mortified for her. Nicky – unlike that to-die-for dreamboat brother of hers – is *SO* not cool.

Mind you, she's harmless. And I'll give her this: she did our class one giant favour when she tipped us the wink about the nitty girl. God, I'd've *died* if I caught lice. Imagine it in my hair? It's so thick, so long.

'Well done, Nicky,' I bigged her up in front of Mags and Jan after PSD. And, fair dos, I meant it.

'Yeah, well done,' agreed Margaret. 'Tagging that crawler with a menshie like *Lousy Lizzie* was skill. Worth Old Groat's punny essay any day.'

'"How ay can be more tactful in future?"' Janet squeaked her tuppenceworth in a perjink Miss Jean Brodie voice. 'What does she means "more tactful"? We *were* tactful.'

'Tactless would have been pinning Lousy Lizzie down and singeing out her wee buggies like this, right, Bella?' Margaret chipped in. Musta been gagging for my praise herself now – I've that effect on everyone – because she flicked open her lipstick ciggie-lighter. Ran its flame along Nevin's parting.

Madre de Dio, Mags was out of order! You could smell poor Nevin's hair scorching. (Or – you bitch, Bella – should I say *frying* in all that natural oil?) I should have stepped in. Nearly did. To give Mags a bloody earful . . . But I took one look at Nevin's brace-face grinning staunch beneath the pain – *Really, Isabella, I'm fine, I'm thick-*

skinned. Trample all over me. You guys are still great. Please let me stay here and talk to you – and I just couldn't bring myself to stick up for her.

Anyway, something more important was bugging me.

'Who the hell's Lousy Lizzie anyway?' I asked Mags and Jan. When they replied with shrugs, I tried Nevin. 'She new?'

'Been here a month,' Nicky said, then she gave this choked sort of laugh, and that smile she was wearing on her face suddenly looked like it was hurting her. She blushed purple as a bruise, turning away to mumble, 'That's not bad going, Bella, coz I was in the same class as you for *three years* before you noticed me . . .'

Ouch!

4
YOUR NAME IS LUKA . . .

Not once in three years did you speak to me, Isabella. I was a norman like Lizzie. Till you set your sights on Luke. Then you clocked me all right.

Well, let's be fair to Isabella. What's *to* notice about me? I've average looks: mid-brown hair, kind of face you'd overlook in a crowd – freckles, blue-ish eyes, the odd zit. Most noticeable feature would have to be the temporary train-tracks taking my speech on a one-way journey from Clear to Mumbling. I'm average intelligence too, cruising in the middle of the middle sets in every subject. In school sports I make the teams but never score goals, never win medals, never walk out as captain . . .

See, nothing remarkable about me to catch Isabella's eye. Apart from my big brother.

Everyone thinks Luke has the WOW factor. He's tall, dark, handsome . . . A tick-all-the-boxes cliché, you must be thinking. But if I also tell you that Luke's looks are the least impressive part of him then you might understand why he's remarkable. Coz Luke's just sussed. One of the good guys, without being the swell-head he could be with looks, brains and personality to burn. He makes time for everyone – from me, his nondescript wee sis, to my mum when she needs toileting in the night if Dad's away. I mean, I know she's my own mum, but I just can't handle that . . .

Luke even made time for Yvonne and Caroline when we hung out. Shy as bushbabies by nature, they'd blush as though a sniper had paintballed their faces in ketchup and lose the power of human speech if Luke came within their sights. That wouldn't faze Luke. He'd natter away as if he understood their starstruck grunts perfectly:

'Gnug.'

'Bloop.'

'Oh, you're going to the pictures, girls. Can I come? Kidding. I know your boyfriends are meeting you there. Looking good!'

Now, if Luke had that effect on Yvonne and Caroline, I don't need to spell out his appeal to the more typical remainder of the fair sex. I could have written a bumper chick-lit doorstop about dames who've stalked Luke, phoned him on redial, fallen at his feet. (Literally, on one occasion, at a school dance where sneaked-in vodka jelly and vomit were involved.) That would have been taking the easy way out, wouldn't it? Diverting you, dear reader, with limpid tales of teenage love. Unrequited teenage love for that matter, because although Luke's one natural born flirt, he doesn't date.

Which is why I was surprised that Luke hooked up with Isabella Della Rosa.

And you were beginning to think Luke just *too* perfect? Well, three months ago they met. *We* met.

And although I've admitted that everything was my fault, I suppose *nothing* would have kicked off if Isabella hadn't charmed the pants off my brother.

This happened in July, early in the summer hols. It was my fifteenth birthday, though I couldn't say the bunting was up outside our house to mark the occasion. But don't be thinking I'm after sympathy when I tell you that. It's just that us Nevins don't go in for pointless celebrations any more. Not with Mum so sick. As Dad says, every day she's still here, not in some bloody institution with a computer for a voice – well, that's as good as a day gets in his book. I'm with him on that.

Plus I'm not exactly deprived in the party stakes. In the Good Old Days – ironically, I'd say now – Mum threw so many hoolies I wonder if she knew her dancing years were numbered. *Any* excuse: her first half-marathon, her last Munro, my half-birthday, Luke's treble at Prize-giving, Dad's latest batch of home-brew ready for drinking, the first cuckoo, a vowel in the month, and Mum could have our house jumping till dawn. *Hey, I fancy having a few people round.*

The wine would flow. Tables would groan with mountains of great grub Mum'd rustle up out of nowhere. In-laws, friends, schoolmates would jam the flat. All welcome. There'd be jigging in the hall. A disco in my room. Uncles and cousins tuning up guitars and fiddles in the kitchen. And at some late hour Mum would always sing. Old folk songs that lured her guests into a silent semi-circle: 'Whiskey in the Jar', 'She Moved Through the Fair', 'My Lagan Love', 'Believe Me If All Those Endearing Young Charms' . . .

It's funny, but the only thing our neighbours ever

complained about in all Mum's party years was her singing. And they still go on about it: *Why didn't she sing more? . . .Why did she have to stop so soon . . .?*

Well, that was then. And now you get the picture why there was no birthday party for yours truly this year. Anyway, Dad was away on the rigs – *Overtime, love. Sorry. Here's forty quid* – and Caroline and Yvonne, still my bezzies back then, were in the middle of their respective Oh Wow! There's a Museum/Graveyard/Cathedral/Fossil walking holidays, and Mum . . . well, this year she was so wiped after a week of *more* pointless tests in some new clinic that Luke had to put her to bed early. Then he took me to this new Italian in the West End.

'Capone's, it's called, Nick. Staff dress up as gangsters.'

Swanky, it looked. Not for the likes of me, I knew, soon as our waitress sashayed up. She gave my new black birthday baggies a right snooty double-take as she showed me and Luke to a booth at the back of the restaurant. Then she slid into the seat beside him.

'*Your name is Luka,*' she sang that Suzanne Vega song in a squeaky, flat voice, peeking up at Luke from the fedora which was hiding her hair. '*And you go to my school.*'

'You're at *my* school?' Luke's eyes were up and down this waitress like a marble in a marble-run. Wearing the widest grin I've ever seen on a human face without surgical intervention, he was taking in her double-breasted pinstripe suit and spats. Beneath the fedora she was made up like a 1930s film star.

'Fourth year. Well, after the holidays.' This 1930s film star offered her hand to Luke. 'I'm Isabella Della Rosa,' she said, rolling the name round her mouth like it tasted of rose creams as well as sounding like them. 'Recognise me now, Luka?'

I probably gasped as well as Luke when Isabella's hair cascaded from her hat, draping itself like a stretching cat over Luke's arm.

'Don't think I've seen . . .' Luke was gibbering, unable to stop shaking Isabella's hand. Didn't stop smiling either, his gaze locked on the eyes flashing back at him. The reflection of the candle between them shot tiger's eye gold streaks through Isabella's pupils.

'But you must know Nicky?' Luke droned, spell-bound. 'You're in the same year. How come she's never mentioned *you*?'

And so Isabella and I were introduced. 'Nicky, *ciao*,'

she smiled, a fleeting frown betraying her attempt to place me. Failing, she smiled even more broadly.

'So Nicky's your *sister,* Luka? I didn't *think* she could be your girlfriend . . . Welcome to Capone's, Nicky. It's my dad's place.' Isabella's smile warmed me now. Kiss. Kiss. 'And drinks are on the house!' she insisted even before Luke said it was my birthday.

While Isabella's papa poured us pink champagne, Isabella hung up her fedora for the evening and cosied close to Luke. After our main course she disappeared into Capone's kitchen, re-emerging with a procession of staff behind her singing 'Happy Birthday' at me in Italian, and a giant ice-cream *torta* blazing with fifteen sparklers.

Before I could camouflage my blushes against the plush velvet of our booth, Papa led me to his dancefloor where he pinned my waist to his belly. On castor-feet he waltzed me so fast to his house band playing 'That Old Black Magic', I thought my eyes had left their sockets and rolled round the back of my head. I kept seeking out Luke to rescue me. But was he watching me dance? Was he wheech!

Luke's head was so close to Isabella's his face was curtained by her hair. I watched them snogging through

Papa's wing mirror all the way home. Don't think Luke came up for air once.

I'd my own share of kisses too, that night. 'You're so great, Nicky,' Isabella said in between triple air *mwahs*. 'Just gotta keep in touch now I know who you are.'

Yeah, sure, I thought. OK, she might have seemed as sweet as the *torta della nonna* she spoonfed Luke, but we'd little to say to each other once she'd admitted she couldn't place Caroline or Yvonne and discovered I sang in the choir.

Yet unbelievably Isabella was on the phone the next morning.

'Time to celebrate your birthday properly, Nicky. I'm taking you clubbing, girlfriend.'

I wasn't dreaming. When I hurried to her house before she changed her mind Isabella was all over me. She'd even bought me a present: this belly-baring, skimpy-strapped number in filmy crimson fabric that slipped through your fingers like liquid silk. Alas, it did nothing for me apart from exposing the undercooked doughnut of flab round my middle where the liquid silk rode up and my jeans cut into my love handles.

It made Isabella look amazing, however.

In the Devil's Den that night she was swamped by so

many guys she didn't speak one word to me till Luke came to collect me.

Then, like magic Isabella was by my side. Holding my hand. Fiddling with my charm bracelet. Telling me how well silver went with freckly skin like mine. She even pretended not to notice Luke until he coughed shyly, most un-Luke himself. Then Isabella drew back her hair to keek a smile at him.

'Nicky and I've had *so* much fun together, Luka,' Isabella said, squeezing me in a hug. 'Isn't she *bellissima* in red?'

'Definitely,' Luke replied. His voice was dreamy. His eyes were not on me.

For three whole weeks that summer Luke was infatuated with Isabella. He dated her any night she wasn't with me.

'You're bewitched, son,' my dad ribbed him. 'This must be some big doll turning your head. Hope I get the chance to see what the fuss is about before the wedding.'

But Dad had nothing to worry about. Isabella's summer spell wore off well before the new school term began.

'So it's *finito*, Luka says. He has to *study*. This is his *big year,*'

Isabella scowled the morning after her final date with Luke. I wouldn't say she was visibly heartbroken. More like black affronted that someone had the nerve to dump her. I'd been summoned over.

Isabella plonked me on her bed. Laid her hands on my shoulders. For one horrible, horrible moment I thought she was going to chuck *me* because Luke had chucked her. Instead she grasped my hands.

'I really need you now, Nicky,' she said, her words wafting round me like a rose-scented summer wind. *Isabella needs me. Really needs me . . .*

'You gotta help me get Luka back. I can't lose him now,' she added urgently. Then, while I bathed in the joy of being wanted by an alpha girl for the first time in my mousy life, she proceeded to ignore me while she yanked every outfit from her wardrobe. There was a new song and dance routine to match every costume change she made in the hour I sat like an invisible nothing on her bed.

'One way, or another, I'm gonna find ya, I'm gonna git ya, git ya, git ya, git ya,'

Isabella snarled as she zipped herself into a two-tone Blondie mini. She must have admired her own ass shaking itself for ten minutes before changing into a full length sequined number and giving it a blast of 'I Will Survive'.

For her finale, at least ten outfits later, Isabella eased herself into a red satin catsuit. Thrusts and grinds of her pelvis were accessorised with her singing: *'I am byoodifool, no matter what he says. Luke. Won't. Bring. Me. Down.'* at the top of her voice.

The encore was Isabella stripped to her underwear. Piling her hair on top of her head, she eyeballed herself in the mirror. I watched as she stroked her fingers across the perfect olive skin of her brow, singing in a breathy but tuneless imitation of Marilyn Monroe: *'I'm gonna wash that Luke back into my hair, and make him BEG for me.'*

Oh, I thought, Isabella was beautiful. If only that could have been enough to keep Luke interested in her. But it wasn't.

'She's a lovely looking girl,' Luke had shrugged when, on Isabella's instruction, I quizzed him about why he'd dumped her, 'but we'd nothing to talk about. She's a dunderheid. Bitchy. Superficial. I could never be serious with her in a million years. Anyway, I'm sticking to my books.'

When I reported back to Isabella, I only quoted

'Lovely looking girl' and 'I'm sticking to my books', sandwiching Luke's statements with a *but*. Massaging the truth, I think it's called. More like protecting my interests. See, I was *desperate* to remain in Isabella's magic circle, letting some of her glamour rub off, gilding my averageness.

So no wonder I was grateful – not to mention pleasantly surprised – when, at the end of her fashion show, she kissed me on both cheeks.

'So, Nicky. Luka wants to play hard to get? OK. I'll just have to make *you* my project instead. When he sees how good I am for his little sister, he'll come running.'

5

JANET

SUN SIGN: CANCER ♋

RULING PLANET: MOON ☽

Cancerians can be crabby and moody.

They have vivid imaginations and cannot always tell the difference between reality and fantasy . . .

'Jeez-Louise, check the wee tag-along from school Bella's brought!' I says to Mags when we turned up at the Devil's Den. There was me with my Tenerife tan and Mags all Benidorm bronzed, pair of us in matching white minis and kiddy-sized vests. All legs and boobs and bare brown backs. Two stoaters. Nearly as good as Bella on a bad night. Ready to break every heart in the Devil's Den between the three of us.

Till we clocked the 'new pal' Bella said we'd 'have' to meet.

'She's in our year. You'll know her when you see her.

Just put up with her for my sake, right?' were Bella's orders.

Bummer!

Mind you, it's not that we weren't used to this carry-on. Bella'd adopt and drop other new pals when it suited her. One was a wee sad-sack two years below us who'd a massive swimming pool in her garden. We spent last summer hanging out with her because it never rained much. Another time Bella hooked up with Poofter Paige's cousin to see what dirt she could dig on his private life. Then before the December exams last year Bella had Mags and I wasting a whole *week* keeping company with Einstein Elaine when we could have been Christmas shopping. Four of us revising together, for God's sake. Three of us still scoring single figures in maths!

So we knew Bella must have good reason for dredging up this lumpy Herbert I half-recognised from the netball team.

'"Nicky who?"' I says when Bella did the formals. Beside me Mags slid her sunnies from the top of her head and put them on to give Nicky a good critical.

'Look how droolicious Bella's got *you* looking,' Mags said, digging me so obviously in the ribs that Nicky Nevin would need to be blind to miss it.

'I couldn't think *who* Bella was talking about when she said you were coming out with us tonight,' I dropped in, mainly coz I was being blinded with the glare from Nevin's metal mouth.

'Well, she hung with the Gerbils before,' Isabella shrugged, as if that explained everything. She slid her own sunnies from her hair and put them on Nicky. While she did it she sucked at her bottom lip with her top teeth.

Me and Mags just about cracked up.

'We're hanging with one of the *Gerbils* –' I started to object, but Isabella cut me dead.

'Nicky's *Luke* Nevin's sister,' she says, winking at me over her shoulder as she led her new pal into the heart of the Devil's Den.

6

CAROLINE

SUN SIGN: SAGITTARIUS ♐

RULING PLANET: JUPITER ♃

Sagittarians admire honesty and justice. They are bright and intelligent, though not always graceful . . .

Until we went back to school after the holidays, Yvonne and I didn't understand what had gone wrong with Nicky. We'd been friends for ten years, never a cross word. Then suddenly Nicky didn't want anything to do with us. Before term started Yvonne and I phoned her loads. Always got Luke, or Mr Nevin. Or the machine. Nicky was never in. She never phoned back.

We began to worry that Nicky might be lying low because Mrs Nevin was sicker. We knew Nicky wouldn't have handled that. Yvonne said we should just go round. Bang on the door.

'We're best friends. She's got to know she *can* talk to us about her mum even though she won't,' Yvonne argued.

I persuaded her not to interfere, in case Mrs Nevin *was* bad and we *were* being nuisances. Glad I did now. Decided to wait till the first day back at school. The three of us would be together again in loads of classes. We'd find out if something horrible had happened to Nicky over the summer.

And something horrible had happened.

Yvonne and I knew it the moment Nicky lifted her hand to wave at us as we hurried across the schoolyard to see her and it was pulled back down by Isabella Della Rosa. We couldn't believe our eyes!

'Quick, Isabella's holding on to Nicky,' I said to Yvonne, but Yvonne – who I'd never, ever heard raise her voice – was already shouting.

'Leave our friend alone, Isabella!'

Grabbing Nicky's free hand, Yvonne tried to tug her from Isabella's hold.

'Come with us,' I said, reaching for Nicky's other arm. The one Isabella held.

But Nicky stepped back. She flicked Yvonne and me away like you'd swipe a moth.

' I'm fine,' she scowled. And there Nicky stood, arm-in-arm with the It girl of Upper School, and her two sarky sidekicks. The four of them, Nicky included, wore matching sneers.

'Oh Nicky, are you sure you don't want to go back to your quiet little playmates, with their blinky pinky eyes and sticky-out teeth?' Isabella asked. She'd her fingers curled into rodenty paws as she stroked pretendy whiskers and squeaked into Nicky's face.

Slowly, deliberately, Nicky shook her head.

'We're the Gerbils,' Isabella squeaked at us loud enough to set big daft Margaret Muir and Janet Pike braying their heads off as they whisked Nicky into the girls' toilets, 'and we're going to be vewwy sad because Nicky doesn't share our nest any more. She's gone to live with Isabella.'

Isabella was right on that score. Spending every weekend her place. So Yvonne and I were told either by Mr Nevin or the clicking on of the answering machine when we phoned Nicky on the first few Friday nights of term.

'Sorry, Caroline, think that daughter of ours is being stolen away from us,' Mr Nevin told me.

'Honestly, I spend less time offshore than Nicky does round here these days,' he complained to Yvonne.

Yvonne and I wondered how Mrs Nevin was coping without Nicky's company. We'd picked Fridays to phone Nicky in the weeks before we gave up trying to speak to her because we knew it was Nicky's Watch With Mother night. Luke always went straight from school to this job he had in a coffee shop, so Nicky had to get home as quickly as she could.

We used to love going back with her. Once Nicky'd loaded her school uniform in the wash the three of us'd sit in her bedroom, each of us doing our weekend homework to get it out the way. Then we'd help Nicky cook dinner. Yvonne always rented out a DVD to watch later with Mrs Nevin, though most nights the four of us just ended up nattering . . .

Wonder if Nicky misses those nights as much as we do?

We could ask her. We *would* ask her, if she would stop looking right through us with this mixed-up look on her face. Yvonne thinks it's panic and unhappiness and fear all jumbled together.

7

GIRLS JUST WANNA HAVE FUN

One of the best things about starting every weekend with Isabella was having a mum to wash my school uniform, even if wasn't my own mum. Signora Della Rosa found my damp, crumpled shirt and skirt drying on Isabella's radiator the very first Friday night of term we went clubbing. When I explained I did my own washing because my mum wasn't fit, Signora Della Rosa cracked up.

'Never bring wet clothes here again, *povera,*' she insisted. '*I* wash your uniform. *Capisce*?'

So now I didn't bother going home on Fridays at all. Left Mum a salad in the morning so my weekend began in Capone's with Janet and Margaret and Isabella.

'Happy Hour' Isabella called it.

Sitting at our special table while the waiters strutted round Isabella, giving her the glad eye if Papa wasn't looking, we'd prop our schoolbooks against the bottles of sweet Lambrusco Papa let us down like lemonade. Any homework would be dashed off, the others copying my answers word for word. Soon as she'd a couple of drinks inside her Isabella would be up 'testing, testing' the house band's mike, and seizing the opportunity of an empty dancefloor to belt out full-throttle versions of 'My Way' or 'Volare'. Once Isabella's set was over we'd gulp a plate of pasta then head back to hers to dress for the Devil's Den.

Three nights in a row we went clubbing. At first I loved it. Not only because it was exciting going out up town in term-time (I'd never done that before unless I could count occasional Saturday night treats to the ballet with Yvonne and Caroline as largeing it). But more than going out I loved the hours we spent whooping 'Girls Just Wanna Have Fun' with Margaret and Janet while I tried on anything I fancied from Isabella's slush-pile of worn-once clothes. With a few strokes of her make-up pencils and brushes, I would transform into some glamorous other me for a few hours. Sometimes I almost had myself convinced as much as the horned bouncers outside the Devil's Den that I was eighteen and gorgeous with it when I catwalked past them in Isabella's shoes, Isabella's gear.

Inside the club I loved being swallowed by its atmosphere. That haze of dry ice, fag smoke, other people's body heat clinging to my skin. I loved the way the ceaseless underfoot BOOM BOOM heartbeat of the music pulsed strong enough to drive me on to the dancefloor. Once out there I found it was impossible to hear what anyone said to me unless I leaned close to my dancing partner, offering myself for a whisper.

I loved that too – oh yeah – the intimate thrill of some stranger's lips shivering those little follicles on my earlobe, the cloud of his cologne swirling in the space between us. *Where do you work? I've seen you here before with that Italian girl. She's a stoater* . . . But even better I liked the way me and my girlfriends – Isabella, Margaret, Janet – would have to huddle with our arms around each other's waists when we'd something to say about someone. No one else on the jampacked dancefloor could hear a word of what our touching heads concealed. It was like having our own little club within a club. Our own little *in*clusive, *ex*clusive coven.

Until, that is, the novelty of dancing round my handbag in Isabella's *Sex And The City* heels began to wane. It was far more of a laugh, I realised, tarting myself up to go than actually *being* there.

While we were dollying up, Margaret and Janet went through this routine, imagining how everyone we knew in the school should dance, or snog. They were so comical – even when they kept doing me, and stuck their bums or their teeth way out – that I'd end up rolling on Isabella's carpet, begging them to stop. Yet once inside the Devil's Den, none of us seemed to have anything funny or interesting to say. You couldn't make yourself heard over the electronic plink-a-plink of dance tracks that all sounded exactly the same. If you wanted to tell the others to watch your drink in case it was spiked when you went off to the loo, you'd to shout yourself hoarse and act out stupid mimes that the others pretended not to understand. It was much simpler, when you weren't dancing, to behave like all the clubbers and pose. Even that was difficult. The Devil's Den was in almost pitch darkness. It was lit by sconces spluttering high on its sweaty walls, and was smoky enough to make my eyes water and my throat burn. Each night we went back there I seemed to be spending longer and longer outside the Fire Door, wishing I'd the taxi fare or the guts to go home.

8

THE MORNING AFTER THREE NIGHTS BEFORE

And I should definitely have gone home last night, I groaned as Isabella rolled me off my sofa-bed on to her floor. Monday morning and I was beginning another school week completely knackered, weekend homework unfinished after three nights on the ran-dan. The furthest thought in my fuzzy head was the return of Lizzie Brownie after her nit sabbatical.

'What you on about? Lizzie who?' I muttered, thinking I was having an interactive nightmare when Isabella hauled me to a sitting position and poured cold slimy liquid over my head and down my jammies.

'That Lousy'll be back in school today.We're not taking chances, Nevin. I've made a potion: conditioner mixed with lice lotion and tea-tree oil. Skinks like boke but nits'll skite off the stuff,' Isabella told me, yanking my hair back.

Combing through it with rough fingers.

'But I wash my hair every morning,' I tried to protest. 'I don't need conditioner –'

'How not, Nicky?' Janet, whose hair was already plastered down and drawn back tight in a roll at the back of her head, caught Margaret's eye in the dressing-table mirror. She winked.

'You're not worried about your hair being greasy?' Margaret asked sweetly. Both of them blinked at their reflections. They looked ten years too old for their school uniforms with their hair up, last night's eyeliner smudging into the bags under their eyes.

I didn't answer that one. Appealed to Isabella instead.

'I'm stinking of smoke. Can't I have a shower?'

'And make us all late, Nicky?' Isabella flung up her arms in exasperation.

I could have had ten showers AND a full Scottish breakfast in the time she spent separating her own potioned hair into long liquorice strands which she pleated, then pinned across the top of her head. Then rearranged. Pleated again. As a finishing touch she doused her head with a can of her mama's industrial strength hairspray.

'D'you think Luka'll like his Heidi, Nicky?' she curtsied when she was *finally* ready for school. 'Too pretty for parasites.'

I was too busy choking from CFC poisoning to join in the others' laughter.

'I like that, Bella. Pretty.'

'Parasites. Are they French nits?'

Nor could I have cared less about catching lice. I was way too knackered. Isabella had kept me awake till dawn retelling her favourite bedtime story. The one about Luke kissing her while I danced with Papa at Capone's. She'd Mags and Jan in hysterics with her impressions of a sad-sack she said was me who waltzed and humphed and stomped round her bedroom with a pillow, tripping over her feet, twisting her head from side to side in a panic.

'"Where's my big brother? I wanna see my big brother!"'

I wanted to see my big brother today as I was whisked to school by Papa. If we'd driven past Luke, I'd've had an excuse to make Papa let me out. I was sick to my empty stomach thanks to the cocktail of Bella's reeking nit potion combined with Papa's wee man in the big motor need to overtake every vehicle on the road.

But I didn't see Luke. Didn't see anyone I knew, unless you count Lizzie Brownie.

Hardly recognised her, only double-taking the figure in school uniform because it was completely bald. Like Sinead O'Connor in that classic 'Nothing Compares 2 U' video where she cries real tears. As I watched Lizzie recede through the car's rear window, her eyes – huge. How come I'd never noticed before? – caught mine just as Papa swerved to avoid a coach parked at the school gates. If his boy-racer driving hadn't thudded Margaret and Janet into my lap and knocked all the wind out of me, I'd have pointed Lizzie out.

Hey, check that! It's baldy bane!

9

YVONNE

SUN SIGN: TAURUS ♉

RULING PLANET: VENUS ♀

Taureans can be shy and cautious.

They make warm, trustworthy friends . . .

Caroline and I couldn't *believe* Miss Groat didn't have something withering to say about Lizzie Brownie's hairstyle – or lack of it. Though as Caroline said, no hair was better than a mane-full of nits. All Miss Groat did was bellow Lizzie to a standstill before she disappeared into school, shooing her on to the idling coach hired to take 4C on our biology field trip. Mind you, maybe Miss Groat was saving her wrath for the four passengers in the red sports car screeching into the schoolyard in a cloud of exhaust smoke. Every pupil in 4C should have been on the coach fifteen minutes ago.

Miss Groat had been most specific.

'8.45am prompt or it's a Friday afternoon detention.'

The coach driver was already pulling away when Margaret Muir (Caroline said it was lucky there was a champion sprinter among the latecomers!) thumped her fists on the door.

'Oi! Wait!'

Isabella strolled in her wake. Giving it her Angelina Jolie pout. Like she was catwalk posing.

'Look. She's modelling her new pleaty hairdo for us,' Caroline nudged me.

I was more interested in the state of Nicky struggling across the yard at Isabella's back. She was trackled with two extra hockey kits as well as her own. Miserable, she looked. None of her new pals hung back to help her, though Janet did snap something that made Nicky jog. Even so, she was last on the coach, just in time to hear Isabella gasp her excuses in one great breath.

'It's totally Nicky Nevin's fault we're late, Miss. Please, Miss. See, Miss. She was staying at mine, Miss, and lost her tie, Miss. Made us all help her look, Miss. Told her we'd be late, Miss –'

Poor Nicky. There was so much hurt written all over her face as she realised Isabella was landing her in it, I could feel my own cheeks throbbing. I was almost relieved when Miss Groat interrupted.

'Not interested in any excuses, dear,' she snarled at Isabella before rounding on Margaret and Janet. 'Show me your insect repellent.'

'Huh?'

'Duh?'

Margaret and Janet blinked, first at each other, then up and down the bus for clues. They weren't even pretending to understand what Old Groat was on about.

'Ladies, I gave clear instructions about this trip last Thursday.' Miss Groat scanned the latecomers. 'With one exception, you were all here,' she went on, before sweeping her beady glare over the rest of 4C.

I tracked it, and noticed it soften to a glance of absolution as it found Lizzie Brownie. She sat alone on the back row of the bus. Staring straight back down the aisle she was. Funny, from where I was sitting her eyes seemed to be fixed on Nicky.

Wonder if I was the only person to notice that? After all, everyone but Lizzie Brownie was concentrating on the power struggle kicking off at the front of the bus where Isabella stroked her cheeks delicately for Miss Groat.

'I couldn't use insect repellent anyway, Miss. Dead sensitive skin, Miss,' Isabella was simpering. When she tossed her pleats at Old Groat she released a waft of chemicals that set everyone within ten rows of her coughing, and poor Caroline rummaging for her inhaler. Isabella's chin was jutting out. There was a challenge in her smirk. You'd think she'd have known better than to argue with Miss Groat. So should Janet and Margaret.

'I'm allergic an' all.'

'Me too.'

Only Nicky was smart enough not to waste her energy. Must have decided it was better to save it for the detention. Triple detention now. She wouldn't be clubbing it this Friday!

'I told you to bring a note if there was any problem, ladies,' Groat dismissed her along with the others. 'And I don't know *what* you're playing at with those hairdos. You'd better hope the insects at Merlock Park are allergic to that smell.'

'We're only keepin' the nits away.'

'You'll not be turnin' up your noses when *your* heads start crawlin',' Margaret and Janet whinnied as Miss Groat finally shooed them to seats and the coach left the school.

'Where is Lousy anyway? Not sitting next to her,' Isabella muttered as she passed me.

'Up the back,' Janet told her.

'Had a radical baldy,' said someone else.

There was a single seat at the emergency door half-way up the bus. It was across the aisle from me and Caroline. That's where Nicky stopped, dumping all the bags she was carrying in the extra space. The day hadn't even started yet and she looked completely wrecked, all this sticky sweat on her face. Big black circles under her eyes. I nearly asked "Y'OK?" but as she turned to sit she rammed a hockey stick into my thigh. I didn't hear any apology so I kept my mouth shut.

10

POND DIPPING

Yvonne completely blanked me when I bumped her leg. I said sorry but she was already studying this handout headed Common Pond Beasties at Merlock Country Park. When I leaned across to ask about it, Caroline shrugged. Turned her head away.

'Better see Miss Groat.'

'Do I smell that rank? Sorry,' I tried, but that got me nowhere with either of them.

And so I passed the rest of the journey not talking to anyone. Several rows behind me Isabella, Janet and Margaret were hell bent on entertaining themselves whether the rest of 4C fancied a morning cabaret or not. Bella took lead vocals in the school trip girrrrls band – natch – and I wasn't invited to join her backing singers. But I wasn't that fussed. Too busy wondering how I'd feel when I was back in Merlock Park again.

* * *

The first time since Mum . . . First time without Mum . . .

When I leaned my head against the window I found I could use the glass like a hologram, to change the things I saw. If I caught its reflection at a certain angle I was staring back at myself. It wasn't an inspiring sight. Isabella had my hair scraped back so tight that my eyes really did look as stretched as they felt. Two bloodshot slits in a face that was rounder than a compass-drawn moon. No wonder I shifted focus beyond myself.

Then I could spy on Caroline and Yvonne. They were scrutinising their Pond Beastie handouts with Einstein Elaine.

'I'd love to see a damselfly nymph.'

'Me too, Yvonne.'

Dead earnest, they were, sitting forward in their seats, arms hooking Elaine's headrest. Before the holidays, if we'd been going on a trip, I'd have been where Elaine was sitting. Now it was like watching Yvonne and Caroline on the telly. Like soap-star mates: utterly familiar, totally unreachable.

When I rolled my forehead away from them and let

my hot temple press the cool window instead, I could see all the way up the bus. Sunk into the furthest corner of the back seat was Lizzie Brownie. My view of her wasn't always clear. She disappeared like an Etch-A-Sketch shaken away if the bus moved into morning sunshine, reappearing if a dappling of shadow lent substance to her reflection. In those moments I knew she was doing what I was doing: using the window as a spyglass. Our actions differed, however, in slight detail.

I wasn't stroking the glass with my extra rubber finger. Nor were my lips running away with themselves. And I don't think I was staring quite as saucer-eyed hard at her as she was at me. Little wonder I avoided her reflection after a while. Lousy was creeping me out, frankly, goggling and muttering like she was *cursing* me or something. Daft idea, I know. Still, I made myself stick to the views out the bus window when it turned from the main roads and began to leave the city for countryside. Even though I knew the journey blindfold . . .

I could even hear Dad's voice as the fields we were passing stretched out to touch the hills beyond.

'That's the magic thing about Glasgow. Twenty minutes in the motor and you leave the hustle and bustle behind.'

'Or half an hour,' I was hearing Mum's voice too now. Her real voice, not the slowed-down slur she spoke in these days, *'and you're down the coast looking out to sea.'*

Until three years ago, every Sunday, when Dad was on-shore, we'd make a day of it. Dad and Luke would do the sarnies while Mum and I packed the wellies and waterproofs. We'd alternate: sea air one week, hills the next.

Funny. When I was wee, we only ever walked Merlock Park if it was too muddy to climb Queensview, too blustery to brave the Gourock esplanade, too icy for the ridges of the Devil's Pulpit.

Mum said Merlock was a jessie walk for Bravehearts like us Nevins. Mainly flat. Dedicated pathways. Signposts everywhere. Proper toilets. Café. Not challenging enough. That was before she started struggling. First it was hills that tired her. Left her shaky. Made her feet too numb to drive home. Then it was the wind that made her breathless. Blew away words before she could find them in her memory. We stuck to walking Merlock every Sunday for a year, our outings getting shorter and slower. The last time we arrived Mum said she felt too wabbit to leave the carpark.

'You Bravehearts go ahead,' she told us. 'I'll sit in the

sun and drink all Luke's lovely hot chocolate.'

We left her waving us off from a picnic bench on a morning just like this one, any chill of a late summer dawn thawing into a roaster as the mercury rose to burn the cold away. We'd set off in fleeces, but by the time we stood round Mum we were sweltered. Sun beating on our heads as she looked up at us from behind her sunglasses. Her words made me shiver to the core.

'Don't know how much longer I'll be walking. It's a pest. They say I'll need a chair soon.'

None of us Nevins had returned to Merlock Park since. Well, why the hell would you choose to revisit a place where bad things happen?

I was away with the fairies at the shock of being here again as Old Groat counted us off the bus. There, on the edge of the car park as the coach drove into Merlock, was the same picnic bench where Mum and her bad news had waited for me. I didn't want to but I couldn't stop looking at it, almost expecting to see the ghost of Mum's old self still sitting there. Or at the very least a brass plaque marking the spot where everything changed for the worse:

IN MEMORY OF THE MUM NICKY NEVIN LOST THE LAST TIME SHE VISITED THIS GODFORSAKEN PLACE.

The heat in Merlock Park felt just as cruel as on that last day with Mum. I could smell it. Hit you like walking into a wall the moment you stepped from the air-conditioned coach. No breeze would budge it. The air was semi-solid with the weight of it, like thickening jelly or setting amber. It trapped everything it touched, concentrating and distorting the sights and sounds and smells of the park, not diluting them into the atmosphere. So children's cries carrying from the adventure playground were piercing shrill rather than distant, and dog crap wafting foul from grass verges clung to my nostrils long after it should have done. The duckpond where Old Groat assembled us shimmered brown like slimy chocolate in a vat, the few ducks cutting trails through its reeds moving as listlessly as they quacked. The sun was liquefying the potion on my head, making it prickle through my scalp and down my face and neck. Into my eyes. My arm was a ton weight when I dragged it across my brow, its surface slick with tiny sweat bobbles clinging to its hairs.

'We're melting,' I heard Janet pant. She was wiping her forehead with her school tie.

'Get us in the shade quick,' said Margaret. She'd the top three buttons of her shirt open, exposing a ravine of cleavage. Old Groat would kill her for that, I thought. But Old Groat was already up ahead, under a huge leafy tree, helping this bloke in a khaki T-shirt and combat shorts dish out plastic tubs and nets and laminated versions of the Common Pond Beasties at Merlock handout I'd seen on the bus.

'Now, you should all have an idea what you're looking for already, 4C,' Groat's words hung so tired in the air I imagined I could see them bobbing past me in a row, like karaoke lyrics, 'and we'll work in our groups of three to collect data. Alan here,' her sucking-a-lemon face forced itself into a smile of introduction, 'is our ranger today. '

'Uh-oh, Uh-oh, Uh-OH,' I heard Isabella sing in her Beyoncé-est voice. From setting off from the bus at a straggle with Margaret and Janet, she'd miraculously slinked to the front of the class. She was now so close to Alan that her Heidi hair was pressed against his chest and he was pressed even harder against his leafy tree.

'Er. First of all, if you could all move back a bit . . .' An unfamiliar voice, softer and curiously higher than Old Groat's, seemed to speak through Isabella's back. Then the ranger's face grinned round her. Took us all aback, I'd say, the gentleness of his manner in contrast to the unsmiling authority of Old Groat. Nobody laughed or anything, though. I suppose because Alan was well fit. Tanned. Toned. Slim, muscley legs like a cyclist. Big friendly smile on his face while he watched Old Groat manhandle us into a semi-circle.

Not – you understand – that I was looking at him in *that* way. With the exception of Peter Gibson ('major geek' according to Isabella), who's had the hots for me since before I could crayon my own name, I've never seemed to attract . . .

But let's *not* go there. This story isn't about me, is it? I'm only saying Alan looked well fit because I was assessing him *scientifically*. Wondering what he had that made Isabella jut one hip towards him at an angle that *must* have killed her back while she swayed hypnotically, sucking at her pinkie. Boobs practically tickling his goatee. Meanwhile Margaret and Janet were risking suspension by unbuttoning their shirts completely then knotting them above the belly.

'Pretty hot today, you guys,' Alan said, seemingly unfazed either by heat or by the sight of Isabella running her tongue round and round her lips, and her index finger up and down her cleavage. He did, however take out a floppy camouflage hat which he pulled down over his eyes.

'Insects are out in force. Midgies, wasps, clegs. Look.' He waved one hand through a moving grey cloud beneath the nearest tree, swatting a bluebottle from his face with the other. His words set Miss Groat fumbling in her handbag for what appeared to be a net curtain. When it was draped over her head she looked like the Bride of Frankenstein.

'Major improvement, Miss,' I heard Margaret mutter. Alan waited for Janet's sniggers to subside before he continued.

'If you think the insects are bad down here, just wait till we walk uphill to the pond where the trees close in. If you've brought repellent, then slap it on. If you haven't,' he grinned round us, 'let's hope you're not tasty.'

'Rules me out then. Coz I'z sweeta than honey, honey,' Isabella giggled behind her hand loud enough for the whole of 4C to hear.

Alan ignored her. 'I'd cover up there,' he waved vaguely at Margaret and Janet, though he wasn't looking at them. He was smiling at the back of the semi-circle.

'You'll be very exposed,' he told Lizzie Brownie, pointing at her baldy. 'Have you brought repellent, or a hat?'

'She *is* repellent,' I heard Isabella snort.

'Have mine, dear,' Miss Groat's net billowed eerily from her mouth as she spoke. She held out a can of the same spray that Yvonne and Caroline were rubbing into their faces hard enough to smear their freckles away.

'I'm fine, Miss. Thanks,' Lizzie said, her voice so clear and confident that everyone in 4C turned to stare.

'You sure? I'm finished with it, dear.'

'Honest, Miss.'

'You sure?' This was Alan. 'These midgies are murder. If I were you I'd . . .'

'I won't get bitten.'

Now here's a weird thing. I'd never heard Lizzie Brownie speak up before. OK, so I'd been there when she answered to her name in class, but I'd hadn't been *listening* properly. As soon as she said *'I won't get bitten'* to Alan, I wanted to hear her talk some more. There was this *quality* to her voice that made you think it couldn't possibly belong to someone like her (I suppose like my mum's disease voice doesn't match her either). Of course Lizzie's voice was nothing like Mum's. It was low yet clear, and slightly husky. I thought it even made her look different. While she was answering Miss Groat, then Alan, she smiled, and I kid you not, her face lit up and I couldn't believe I'd never noticed her before. What I'm saying – and don't be thinking it's because I'm dykey or anything – is that Lizzie Brownie was suddenly beautiful. Not in a bling-bling Isabella way. I mean, Lizzie was pale, really pale now with all her hair shaved, but her eyes, fringed by dark, dark lashes, seemed huge. They flashed green and smiley at Alan and Old Groat, her stare direct. Confident like I could never be.

So confident that Isabella spat, 'Trampy slut.'

So confident even Old Groat didn't argue with her.

Leaving Alan, his eyes lingering on Lizzie's smile to grin, 'Whatever,' for the pair of them, Groat ordered us into our threes behind him as he led 4C uphill.

Of course, muggins here had missed Groat's earlier get-into-groups instruction. Must have happened when I was staring at the picnic bench, three years back in time, seeing Mum there, still able to walk, able to speak properly. I was one of two leftovers bringing up the rear of 4C. Guess who the other one was?

'You two make a pair,' Old Groat told me and Lizzie Brownie.

Alan yomped us uphill on a rain-starved pathway, dust clouding our tramp tramp feet. There were moans and puffs and groans at the pace, although one 4C gal seemed to have enough energy to combine chit-chat with hearty singing. First Isabella entertained Alan to a medley including 'Climb Every Mountain', Kylie's 'Slow' (in a creepy high voice), followed by 'Follow the Yellow Brick Road' in an even creepier everybody-join-in Munchkin voice. When the concert was over Isabella's voice still carried all the way back to Lizzie Brownie and me.

'In case you're wonderin' about the pong, Alan, it's nit killer, Alan,' Isabella explained, 'because see that baldy one, Alan? Right, she was pure *crawlin'* last week, Alan. I'd die if we caught anything from her, so I made up a concoction just in case. Sure it'll kill all the bugs out here, too, Alan?' she yattered, though I didn't hear any reply.

Alan had jogged a few strides ahead of us all,

interrupting Isabella to ask if any of us knew what the hill we were on was called.

'A bugger,' I heard Janet pant while Alan gathered us round him on the edge of the still pond at the top of the high ground.

'No, Gallow Hill actually,' he chuckled, pointing back the way we'd all come. Then he grew serious. 'Just be thankful you're only coming up here for a field trip in the heat.'

Anyone who was lucky enough to have one of the laminated handouts Alan dished out earlier was fanning the air furiously at this point. All movement stopped, however, when Alan nodded at the ground behind him.

'They used to hang people here in the seventeenth and eighteenth century. Thieves, cattle rustlers, petty criminals. They'd bring them up from Merlock Castle. Look. See that turret down there?'

Everyone in 4C squinted through the trees surrounding us towards the black ruin looming in the distance. Everyone except me. Truth be told, I was trying not to look at that dank, miserable ghost of a place. Last time Mum had actually *walked* through Merlock with me and Dad and Luke she'd needed to perch on one of the old castle's tumbledown walls for ages, even though it was pouring that day. She'd hunched forward, head low, rain pelting down her neck. Done in. Legs shaking. Dad had sat beside her, rubbing his hand in an endless circle over her back. *Swoosh. Swoosh. Swoosh* went his palm against her wet waterproof, the pitch and patience of the sound he made putting me into a strop. *What's wrong with you, Mum?* I'd shouted and I think I even stamped my foot when Dad made Luke take me off to explore the castle grounds.

I'm not exploring this dump! I'm soaked and it's ten minutes back to the car park. Mum can walk that! I'd ranted. Then, as I recall, something I hadn't planned to say just came out my mouth. *Anyway, I don't like it here. This place really gives me the creeps . . .*

No. I didn't want any reminders of Merlock Castle, though I couldn't help being interested when Alan started explaining you could still see the dungeons in its grounds. I'd walked over them that day not knowing they were there. No wonder I'd been spooked.

'All sorts of folks would be thrown in there,' Alan said. 'Real crooks mixing with women and children whose only crime was poverty. Everyone would be sleeping on the same floor. No privacy, no dignity, and after a while prisoners would be taken out for trial on this scrubby wee knoll beside the castle. It they were found guilty they'd be brought here to hang. A permanent gallows stood on this hill, hence the name.'

'So are people buried . . .?' Einstein Elaine's question dwindled to nothing as she scanned the area of grass and trees behind us all.

Alan nodded. 'Well, it certainly feels like it when you're here on your own, or at night.' He tapped the toecap of his boot into the water. I watched the slow ripples he'd made radiating over the black surface. Dozens of water creatures, disturbed by the movement, skittered or hopped or darted from view. Hovering above them, all manner of insects swarmed. The air droned and clicked and sweltered.

'And this stretch of water wasn't always used for pond-dipping.' Alan hunkered down now, so the only way you could see his face was in reflection. Rippling. Features distorted by the water. His voice was so quiet that we all leaned in to hear what he said next.

'This is a Drowning Pond. They used to swim so-called witches here. Tied them up. Threw them in. If they drowned, they weren't witches after all.'

'And if they didn't drown, Alan?' Isabella was in there first with the question we must all have been thinking.

Alan stood up, clasping his hands to his neck.

'Werrit till they were nearly dead,' he said, 'then burned.'

I felt a shudder go through every girl in 4C. Beside me Lizzie Brownie gave a tiny cry like something sharp had jabbed her, though no one said a word except Isabella.

'Haggard,' her smile flashed. She sank down to trail her fingers back and forth across the surface of the water. Eyes wide on the ranger's face. *'Tell me more, tell me more,'* she sang, fluttering her eyelashes.

'Well, our maps mark *this* pool as the Drowning Pond though there's another spot that *I* personally think was the real site of any swimm –'

'Fascinating, I'm sure,' Old Groat interrupted, looming over Alan so he actually veered backwards, and nearly fell into the water, 'But we'd better get dipping before one of my girls passes out.'

'Or gets eaten alive,' murmured Margaret.

I'd noticed her scratching herself while Alan was talking, all the way up both of her shins and round her neckline. Janet was doing much the same, only leaning backwards, tearing at her bare calves and the roll of flesh bulging between her skirt waistband and knotted shirt. The pair of them were also doing what I was doing: poking around their slicked-down hair, digging in exactly – I recalled – as Lizzie Brownie had done before I grassed her up last week. I tried to quit scratching myself, but it was impossible. Nipping like mad, my scalp was, and buzzing from flies and wasps that kept diving-bombing to investigate the smell and sticking there. Einstein Elaine had started scratching too, index finger working round her chin. Her face, like fellow group members Yvonne and Caroline, was slowly measling with red weals. She couldn't leave herself alone. None of us could, I realised, watching the rest of 4C spread out to take up dipping positions around the edge of the water. There was a constant twitching/jerking/swatting/raking going on. It must have looked totally bizarre to Old Groat and Alan, this body-popping Justin Trousersnake routine. No wonder after twenty minutes of dipping all our little plastic tubs were free of pond life, and no one had identified a single beastie. Except in my group.

Lizzie Brownie. Well, wasn't she just working away

quite the thing, trailing her net gracefully back and forth at arm's length? Humming while she did so. She made good use of both hands to keep her grip steady because, unlike myself, she'd no need gouge at ten crawling patches of skin once every five seconds.

'We've a water flea, a whirligig beetle, a couple of newts and . . . a pond skater,' she smiled at me, tipping a wriggling insect from her net to our tub. Its movement set me wriggling myself, flapping and jerking so hard at the midgies and clegs round my face that I knocked my clipboard into the pond.

'That is IT, 4C!' boomed Miss Groat, hearing the splash. Hooking the soggy clipboard out with her net she scowled, 'What is the matter with you all? Ants in your pants?'

No one laughed. Everyone was too busy scratching to care that Groat was on the warpath, a lampshade with attitude in her midgie net, stomping along the water's edge to see what we were all up to.

'Not *one* creature in your tub, Elaine. That's not like you, dear. Keep still, Yvonne. Cover up your arms if they're being bitten. Stop *scratching*, girl. You're making it worse, Janet. Get your net in there and dip this pond!'

'Not doing too well here, you guys.' I heard Alan's

voice, though I couldn't place him at first. He'd wandered beyond the pond itself to this little rise of ground above it. Dank and sunless, it was pocked with a circle of stunted trees and withered shrubs. I couldn't think why he'd climbed up there, where there was no water to dip. Until I spotted Lizzie Brownie up there too. For some reason she was in the middle of this lifeless circle (weird, I'd have sworn she was at my side two seconds ago . . .) staring down on us all, hands clasped across her chest like she was suddenly cold. And her mouth was working like she was talking to herself again. Alan was beckoning her back.

'Hey, the ground's boggy up there, and it stinks of rot. You're probably stepping over dead birds and squirrels. You're in a horrible spot. Come down,' he urged her, swimming his hands to part the midgie cloud that haloed him as he strolled to rejoin the rest of us.

'See what I've caught, everyone,' Alan said. He was following Lizzie with his eyes, frowning as she picked her way from the rise to the edge of the Drowning Pond again. 'See, a water scorpion,' he said, still tracking Lizzie. 'And pond skaters. Gather round and have a look,' Alan said.

'I've caught pond skaters, too.'

There was that voice again. Clear through the droning heat. Lizzie was holding out her tub to Alan. I noticed her hand was trembling slightly, that extra finger of hers poking from the side actually, hideously *vibrating*. Looked just like the red-tailed maggot on my laminated card, I thought, nudging Janet and making sure her eyes followed the direction of my head: Check *that* out. Gross, innit?

I watched Janet clock the finger.

Alert Margaret.

Who whispered to Isabella.

Here was something else I'd noticed about Lizzie that I'd be able to bitch about with the others, I thought. And I smiled to myself, even though my arms were itching so badly I'd drawn blood.

'Wow!' Alan frowned as he clocked not just me, but everyone digging nails into livid flesh. 'I've never had a group react like this up here. Let's call it a day.'

'I'm fine,' a lone voice stopped Alan before he could lead us all down Gallow Hill.

'Hey, you *have* done well,' smiled Alan, swirling Lizzie's tub gently. 'Everyone take a quick look at this. There's a freshwater louse in there.'

'So Lizzie's found her long-lost twin.'

I don't know if Isabella meant the whole class to hear her remark, but the air was so still and heavy that every sound carried and we all turned round. Boy, oh boy, she didn't look so hot, her forehead contoured with raised blotches under her Heidi plaits, which had all unravelled in sticky loops. Her eyes, two rheumy slits beneath swollen lids, glittered in Lizzie's direction. Her ear lobes – which she couldn't leave alone – were seeping blood.

'Good grief, Isabella!' said Miss Groat, flinging back her bridal veil to take a better look. 'Your forehead's up like a relief map of the Himalayas!'

'I've antihistamines you can take if you've brought a consent form,' offered Alan, peering into Isabella's face as if she was a specimen of particularly unpleasant pond-weed. Not the way males generally inspected her. No wonder she turned her back on him, scowling.

Of course five pupils hadn't handed in forms. That would be me, Margaret, Janet, Isabella. And Lizzie Brownie. I heard Groat explain to Alan that she would sign for the bald girl *in loco parentis.*

'In between guardians. *Difficult circumstances,'* she summarised neatly for me so I wouldn't forget when I reported to Isabella.

Not that Lizzie needed a form, or antihistamines.

'And that's well weird, innit?' I put to Isabella.

We'd nabbed the back seat of the bus on the way back to school.

'We're bitten alive but not one insect came near her . . .'

'Gonna shut up about insects, Nevin,' Isabella snapped, pressing her hands to the welts on her brow, and shifting a seat away from me. 'You never know when to zip your trap.'

'But you'd think she was in a protective bubble,' I persisted half to myself as I stared up the bus at Lizzie's bald head. She'd replaced me in the single seat I'd taken on the journey to Merlock.

'Drop the subject, Nevin,' Isabella growled, flapping me away. 'Don't wanna think about that place again in my life. Or Lousy Lizzie. Freaky little *witch*.'

11

ISABELLA

SUN SIGN: LEO ♌

CONFLICTING SUN SIGN: PISCES ♓

Appearances really matter to Leos . . .

Madre de Dio. Drop the *bloody* subject, thought I made it crystal to Nevin on the bus. But did the desperate-to-be-loved-one pay any heed? She must have thought *Drop the bloody subject* was code for *Hey, special girlfriend, why not show up after school to obsess about the one topic I'm trying to forget*?

Bet she ran all the way too, *desperate* to fill me in on *everything* I'd missed in a day.

Like I cared!

Christ, she was peeing her drawers from the excitement of seeing me.

'Hi, Isabella. How you doing? I was just passing. Awful quiet in school today with you and Jan and Mags sick. Think you'll be off all week? Everyone else's face is fine today but ooooh, hope you don't mind me saying, yours looks *reeeeellly* sore . . .'

Jeez Louise! Coulda killed Mama for letting Nevin up to my room. OK, so Nicky's as harmless as a summer cold, and I reckon my chumminess with her is still my best bet for winning back an Access All Areas to her brother. But man, she's wearing. Even on a good day I can only take her in small doses: when I'm in the mood, when Mags and Jan are there to water down the Nicky nerdiness and take the piss. I did NOT want to entertain Nevin when my face was a car crash, and I was completely spaced on Piriton and Papa's sleeping tabs to try and make up for the zeds I lost last night thanks to the totally actually *hideous* state of my skin.

But there Nevin was. Fit to burst. Arse blocking my view of Extreme Makeover, she was giving it all this smiley-smiley *How are you, Bella? Let's talk about insect bites to cheer you up, Bella.*

To make matters worse, from what I could see of Nevin's big Scottish Cheddar of a face, she'd not one bite in sight. Talk about seeing her far enough!

Last thing I needed was a sad-sack burbling all the goss from school to impress.

Well, I'm sorry. I just wasn't interested. And I laid it on the line with her. Or so I thought. Look, Nicky, why would I wanna hear you tell me, *'Honest, Isabella, that freaky Lizzie Brownie's the only entire girl in the 4C with no bites on her skin. D'you not think there's something pure dead creepy about her? I do.'*

No, and frankly I didn't think wee Lousy was any creepier than Nicky was being about this whole carry-on. And I didn't *give* anyway. I only cared that *I* was looking like I'd been cutting up cherries and sticking them on my face for a laugh, and that all my bites were leaking ooze and multiplying, and that I of all people couldn't be seen in public looking so totally actually hideous.

'Please don't take me asking you not to visit personally, Nicky,' I said, 'but I don't even want Mags or Jan seeing me till I'm better. And they're my best pals. So if you wouldn't mind pissing off . . .'

Clearly, I was just being far too nice because didn't our Nicky show up same time *next* day. Some folk just can't take a *hint*.

'Gosh! Your face is even *more* swollen today, Bella. The bites look as it they're turning into spots.'

At least I managed to keep her outside my bedroom

door. Gave Mags and Jan time to hide in my wardrobe.

Straight away Nevin was back on her specialist subject: The Fascinating World of Lizzie Brownie. How Lizzie's school uniform was dirty and smelly and frayed. How she was *really* weird. Because I could hear Mags and Jan farting in my wardrobe at this point and chanting,

'Pot.'

'Kettle.'

I didn't pay much attention. Too busy coughing to disguise the racket those jokers were making upstairs. I just nodded, tried not to laugh. Willed Nevin and her wee hang-dog coupon to scram, because – I'm sorry – I just couldn't take any more from her, lurrvly Luke's sister or not. *She* was the one being weird, not Lousy. Leaning in towards me. Tapping the side of her schnozzle.

'You know what, Bella? I think Lizzie's got it in for us because we embarrassed her about the nits. And coz you slagged her the most, your skin's the worst, Bella. Think about it –'

Well. Enough already! Give Nevin any more rope and she'd be suggesting wee Lizzie had *magic* powers or something.

'Nicky, I never wanna think about Lousy or insects or bites or that bloody park again. Thinking makes me itch, itching makes me scratch, and scratching could scar me for life. Anyone would think you're jealous that I've got the looks to make it in showbusiness and you don't want my face to get better. Please go away now,' I said. Shut the door in Nevin's face.

Didn't even care if she heard the applause coming from inside my room, especially when she showed up *again*. We were at Thursday now.

Madre de Dio, was Nevin over her sell-by mate-date already!

'Oh dear, Bella. Has a doctor seen your face yet?' she greeted me when I finally answered the front door. That girl is all tact!

And her observations were *not* what I needed since I'd been up for the third night in a row scratching my face raw. I'd spent a morning in Casualty with smelly people. I'd been referred to a dermatology clinic as an emergency. I was on antibiotics for *acne*. *ACNE*!

'Look,' I told Nevin, when she tried to bombard me with all this claptrap about cradle songs and witches. 'I'm sure the Gerbils'll have you back for a few days if you're that desperate. Go prattle to *them* about what Lizzie did during music. Tell *them* you think she put a curse on us all.

'Go on. Scram!'

12

SONG OF THE CHANGELING

Go talk to the Gerbils, Isabella told me.

Easier said than done even if I wanted to. That week after pond dipping when Isabella, Margaret and Janet were absent I hung about in school like a fart in a trance. Nobody – not one of my old friends – came near me.

Believe me, if it's never happened to you it feels horrible when no one wants to speak to you. You just want to slink away and die. Of course, in my heart of hearts I knew it was my own fault that old friends like the Gerbils cold-shouldered me now.

I was in Isabella's circle and that meant I'd made myself exclusive. So exclusive in that friend-free week Isabella was absent I ended up paired in music with the other odd sock of 4C, Lizzie Brownie.

On reflection, given the heinous state of Isabella's skin that week, it was probably a good thing that Isabella told me to piss off and shut the door in my face when I tried to tell her about Lizzie and the music lesson. You see, in a backhanded way, anything I had to report involved paying Lizzie a compliment. That would not have gone down well with someone whose face had turned into a pepperoni pizza.

That's because . . . I don't quite know how to put this . . . but my new music partner, for all she was creepoid and weird with her rubber finger and charity shop school kit, had the most *amazing* singing voice I'd ever heard. Isabella *definitely* wouldn't have appreciated me telling her that. *She* took private singing lessons so she could apply to stage school in London, although her voice – and I'd *never* tell her this to her face – wasn't that hot. She was one of these swoopy singers with too much tremolo on the high notes. More volume than tone. Whitney meets Mariah meets Celine and all a bit off-key is the easiest way to explain Isabella's sound, that *Titanic* dirge being her party piece. Mrs Jackson cracked up with folk in the choir who sang like that, not that Isabella would have been seen dead in any school choir.

Anyway, this is what happened that Thursday in music,

the morning Mrs Jackson handed out this old Scottish folk song.

It was one I knew well. Hadn't heard it for years, but as soon as I read the first verse, my mum's voice – my mum's *old* voice – crooned in my head.

I left my baby lying here
Lying here
Lying here

'This is a very beautiful song, yet it reflects a dark theme in Scottish folklore. It's more a lament than a lullaby,' Mrs Jackson explained, while Mum accompanied her in my mind's ear.

I left my baby lying here
And went to gather blueberries . . .

'People used to believe that if you didn't show respect for the *sithean*, the fairy folk, you'd fall under their curse and all sorts of evil could happen. You'd get sick, or your crops could fail. Worst of all, the *sithean* might steal your child. It would become a changeling and you would never see it again. That's what this song is about. Anybody know it?'

Only one hand in 4C went up, and before you get any ideas, it wasn't mine. Maybe once I'd have volunteered, especially for Mrs Jackson. Nowadays though, to hang with Isabella, I'd to look as if everything going on in class was bo-ring the arse off me. So all I did was glower at Lousy Lizzie Brownie for sooking up to Mrs Jackson.

'Does it go like this, Miss?' Lizzie said and before Mrs Jackson could say yay or nay, she was singing.

Goran goran gory-o-go
I lost my darlin' baby-o . . .

Lizzie's voice was pure without being shrill, clear without being sweet, full without being loud. I could tell it reached everyone yet weirdly I felt Lizzie was singing to me alone. Her voice made the hairs on my arms stand up like the first time I heard Annie Lennox sing 'Here Comes the Rain Again', or Nina Simone start up 'Feeling Good'. Ran a shiver of fingers down my spine as tingly as Aretha Franklin building up the vocal of 'I'll Say A Little Prayer' or Natalie Merchant reach the chorus of 'Motherland'.

Brought tears to my eyes, like Billy Holiday putting her heart and soul into 'Strange Fruit'. Stopped me in my tracks basically, same as when Dad played Karen Carpenter singing 'Goodbye to Love'. I can't tell you why Lizzie Brownie's singing made me feel the way it did. All I know is that there was more than a song being sung here. There was a story coming true. A reaching back into folklore. A believing in the powers of the *sithean*. And an understanding.

Now if you've kept up with me so far, I wouldn't blame you for thinking I've lost the plot, havering all pseudo about a singer and a song. But believe me, this is important: I'm trying to get across the significance of hearing Lizzie sing . . . And I knew then and I know now that what I heard in that music lesson was something I'd remember for the rest of my life.

When Lizzie came to the final line of the song – *I've lost my darlin baby-o* – she exhaled the words in the saddest whisper. Her eyes remained closed when she stopped singing, her deformed hand drawing the chorus to a fade then settling in her lap. She sat still, head bowed in a roomful of silence. Every mouth in 4C was open, slightly parted. Everyone was blinking, looking about them as if they'd wakened from a dream.

'How beautiful. Thank you,' gasped Mrs Jackson, her hands clutching her chest. 'Where did you learn the song . . . Elizabeth?' she asked, checking the register with a frown.

'My granny used to sing it,' Lizzie shrugged. 'Always known it.'

'I think you deserve a round of applause,' said Mrs Jackson, conducting us to put our hands together, 'and if you don't join my choir today,' she smiled, 'I'm resigning.'

We took our lead from Mrs Jackson, of course. Applauded politely. A spatter of handclaps. But d'you know, something rang hollow in our praise. I mean, a singer *half* as good as Lizzie would earn a standing ovation, cheering, footstomping. Encore! Bravo! She deserved it – and you'll know by now how hard that is for me to say, so it must be true – because her voice was better than any singer I'd ever heard. On stage. On disc. On radio. Yet by singing up in class like that Lizzie'd done herself no favours although I don't think for one moment that she'd sung to show off. What I'm trying to say is that she'd exposed herself as someone even *more* different than she was already.

'I mean, I thought her voice was magic, but I was

blushing hearing her sing up like that.'

'What a brass neck.'

'None of us would be so forward.'

'Too right!'

'Doing a solo like that.'

'Don't think she knew she looked off the wall. She just can't be savvy.'

'Definitely a bit odd.'

This was what I heard when I eavesdropped on Yvonne, Caroline and Einstein Elaine as they post-mortemed the first period of double music down the bogs.

I ached to join in their conversation. *There's something really freaky about Lizzie, isn't there? Have you seen her finger? Wonder why she's fostered. She mumbles to herself.* But I daren't show myself, scared that if I came out my cubicle, my old pals would freeze me out and I'd have to slink away from them, Fanny Friendless. End up reading the school noticeboard again to look busy. Like I'd been at the start of this lunch break. When I'd been joined by the other dropped stitch in 4C.

'Hiya. Wasn't music *FAN-tastic?*' Lizzie had greeted me all smiles, a banana sandwich in her dodgy hand. I tell you, if there's one sight I hate, it's mushed bananas. Especially coating someone's teeth when they say *FAN-tastic.*

'It's good we're partners. You're really into singing. I can tell,' Lizzie banana-breathed. 'Maybe we could practise together if we're in the choir, coz I've never been in a choir before. It's Nicky, isn't it?'

Hold the bus, I was thinking, doing a sideways shuffle away from the noticeboard. Practise my singing with you, hen?

I pointed to the toilets, clutching my belly. 'Gotta go,' I gasped.

'See you back in music, then, Nicky.' Lizzie touched the sleeve of my blouse with her finger. 'Keep you a seat.' If she noticed my shudder she didn't let on.

'Wonder what we'll be doing after lunch?' she asked, her smile squeezing a little worm of banana out the side of her mouth.

'Not sitting beside you for starters, honey,' I muttered.

13

ISOBEL GOWDIE

That first lesson after lunch can be a killer, especially if you're following double pizza and chips with double maths. No chance of a digestive siesta in Lisa Marie aka Mr Presley's class, but music day afternoons are bliss. Mrs Jackson calls the second period of double music our Listen and Absorb time, and actually *instructs* us to close our eyes!

Like any of us ever need to be told twice!

'Just tune in,' Mrs Jackson lilts. 'Even if you sleep you'll be listening subconsciously.'

Is that cool teaching or what? And today, because we'd learned the Scottish cradle song first period, I was looking forward to a wee snoozy.

Nae luck. Although I thought I was on to a winner at first.

'You're going to hear another Scottish piece. Its composer described it as a requiem,' said Mrs Jackson. With a contented sigh I settled my back into my chair, wishing I'd brought a blow-up cushion for the back of my head.

Requiems. Fairly quiet affairs. Well, the ones I'd heard so far. Mrs Jackson had played us Fauré's and Mozart's. We'd to compare them for homework afterwards so I'd spent ages with my thesaurus finding similes for *sublime* and *moving* and *elegiac* to use in the three paraphrased versions of my essay I produced for Isabella, Margaret and Janet.

At least homework would be a scoosh tonight with the others on sickies. Or so I thought as I watched Mrs Jackson dust this afternoon's CD tenderly with her hippy skirt like it was some priceless artefact. Mags and Jan always aped this ritual from the back row, switching off as the music came on, leaving me to Listen and Absorb then do their homework for them. Today, with them absent, I had no distractions. Which is why I was actually disappointed when Mrs Jackson said there wouldn't be any music homework.

'Bit of a challenging piece today, so I want you to work in twos with your neighbour,' she said, 'and discuss what might be happening in the music.'

'Ooooh, I'm with you again, Nicky,' said Guess Who,

digging her elbow into my side like we were *meant* to be together. Heinous! Clearly Lizzie Brownie was one of those people who just can't sense when they're unwanted.

'Great,' I flat-toned, breathing shallow in anticipation of the puff of unwashedness I was sure Lizzie's tatty uniform was giving off. She side-scraped her chair as close to me as it could get.

'Wonder what we'll hear? Should I take notes?' She was practically panting in my face with excitement.

'Whatever,' I shrugged, watching Caroline and Yvonne balance one notebook between them to my left. Beyond, Einstein Elaine was teamed with Peter Gibson. Their knees were touching.

How cosy.

And here was me . . . landed.

This totally actually hideous situation meant I was too busy studying the stains Lizzie's school skirt had absorbed to concentrate on listening to anything Mrs Jackson was saying. My ears only pricked up when I heard her mention a familiar name.

'. . . be hearing some modern classical music: *The Confession of Isobel Gowdie* by James Macmillan.'

Isobel, I thought. Another excuse for reporting to Bella straight from school. Hey, you've a piece of music named after you. Right up her street that would be.

Though maybe not if Isabella knew what had happened to her namesake.

'In 1662, Isobel Gowdie was tortured until she confessed to being a witch,' Mrs Jackson, explained. 'She was strangled then burned. Listen.'

I don't know what I was expecting when the music started. Soaring choirs? An orchestra in harmony? To be honest, I wasn't even switched on the way I usually try to be in music. I was too riled by the unselfconscious way Lizzie hunched forward in her chair with her freakoid hand actually *cupping* her ear like one of the Arran-jumpered Irish folksingers Luke and Dad have a fondness for. No one sat like that. We were all more or less upright, arms folded. Being normal. *Not sticking out like a deformed pinkie,* I glowered at my partner, wishing her nothing but misfortune.

Which is why I took longer than usual to settle into *The Confession of Isobel Gowdie*. Missing the soft sad opening strings, I only focussed when these same strings produced sounds you couldn't ignore: scraping noises that made me shiver as if someone was scoring metal tines down my back. Setting my teeth on edge. After that it was impossible not to listen whether you wanted to or not. You couldn't exactly drop off when rat-a-tat snare drums were jumping you out of your skin and violins and cellos were mimicking a hammer driving in nails somewhere you daren't think about: a gibbet at best, but more likely a leg bone. I'm no expert, but I'd never heard anything so full of danger and evil in music before.

I wasn't the only one.

Can't *ever* remember such a buzz after Listen and Absorb. Usually we're all too zapped on melody to volunteer any thoughts and Mrs Jackson goes round us all one by one, skipping anyone who's in the Land of Nod. But no one was sleeping today.

'What was *that* all about?'

'Bits of it weren't like music at all.'

'Miss, some of that reminded me of *Psycho*. Y'know the *ee ee ee* when the dagger's coming down in the shower scene?'

'Did anyone hear feet skittering about as if someone's being chased?'

'No, that was meant to be dancing.'

'Look, my hands are sweatin'.'

'My heart was thumping when all those drums were rattling like that.'

'That was the scariest –'

'Hey.' Mrs Jackson banged her tambourine, a cue for silence. 'You're meant to be working in twos,' she said. 'Mr Jackson's hoping you'll all write wonderful essays in English tomorrow inspired by what you've heard today. So brainstorm everyone,' she trilled, her voice rising an octave above our collective groan. There was *nothing* of Mrs Jackson's chilled-out lovebeads and cheesecloth vibe in her old man Jacko's teaching methods.

The volume of the hubbub around me shrank to a non-stop muttering, its intensity, I shivered, recalling the chattering sounds in the music we'd just heard. Everyone was whispering to a neighbour, heads close, animated, exchanging murmured ideas. Only Lizzie and I remained silent.

I hadn't looked at her since the music finished although I knew I'd have to do it soon, before Mrs Jackson pulled me up for skiving.

'That was *terrifying,*' Lizzie whispered at last. I

presumed she'd taken the reluctant turn of my head as a nod to share her opinions – like I cared. I was wrong, however. Lizzie was talking to herself again.

'I felt as if someone was after *me*. There were stabbing sounds,' she went on, eyes widening. Man, talk about getting into the music! Lizzie's voice was quavering.

'. . . And I could imagine a mob hunting Isobel down. Grabbing her. Dragging her away to be tortured. She's praying. Begging for her life . . .'

Now I noticed that Lizzie's hands, as she crossed them over her chest and throat, were trembling.

'I could *see* it all happening. Did you, Nicky?' Lizzie asked, green eyes finally meeting mine.

Of course I did, I thought as I looked away.

Well, come on? Did you think I was going to *admit* to Lousy Loser Lizzie that I thought the gentle theme beneath the cacophony of the piece was heartbreaking? That listening to *The Confession of Isobel Gowdie* carried me back to the Drowning Pond in Merlock Park?

Don't be ridiculous.

'Dunno,' I shrugged when Lizzie asked if I thought the quiet music was Isobel pleading her innocence, and everyone just ignoring her.

'Whole thing just sounded like an orchestra tuning up to me. Pish,' I lied, as Mrs Jackson rattled her tambourine for attention and the period bell rang.

Truth be told I *do* wish I could have talked to *someone* leaving the Music room about how I felt. Caroline. Yvonne . . . They'd have been perfect. Just to dismiss the Merlock/Isobel Gowdie connection as daft and to delete the picture I had in my mind's eye of Lizzie Brownie staring down at me from that boggy circle of dead trees while we were pond dipping. Hands to her throat. Shaking.

14
SMEDDUM

Luke kept promising me English would be a hoot this year.

'Having both Jacksons is great, Nick. There'll loads of overlap between English and music. You'll write blues lyrics and set Shakespeare to music. It'll be fun.'

I'm sure English was fun when you were Jacko's top dog, like Luke, but I wouldn't say there'd been many side-split moments in 4C, unless you saw the funny side of grammar revision and non-stop interpretations. I certainly didn't. And I hadn't experienced any chucklicous English/ music overlap up to now either.

In fact I'd started dreading English. Jacko had been coming down hard on me ever since I'd clocked up an impressive C-minus in the last interpretation I fired off tipsy on three tumblers of Lambrusco in Capone's.

'You can do considerably better, Nicola,' Jacko had warned when he handed my paper back with a disappointed tut. 'I don't want to be bothering Mum so early in the term, so you'd better *screw the nut*, what? Let's begin by extricating you from your cackling coven at the back of the class, and set your smiling countenance where I can see it properly.'

He always went on like this, did Jacko. Adored big doughy sentences plump with fancy words. He was all right though, him and his matching pocket hankies and bow ties, if bloody hard on skivers.

Which is why I though I'd be in for it when I arrived late for his Friday class, having sloped off to the bogs after French to lose Lizzie. See, she'd hung back looking as if she planned to cleek me to English. Like, in your dreams, loser.

By the time I slipped into Jacko's everyone else was already seated, and the room was quiet.

Expecting a detention, or a bawling out at least – *Explain your tardiness, young lady!* – I couldn't believe my luck! No bollocking. Jacko frowned, right enough, flicking out his pocket watch, before beckoning me to a seat at the front of his class.

'Head down. Listen, Nicola,' he whispered, miming his instruction then sweeping his arm around the class to show me what he meant as if I was a total retardo. And there was a strange sight. Everyone in 4C lolling across their desks, heads on arms. Bizarre, but a lot more fun than coining metaphors. I cheered up, scraping out the only spare chair in the front row.

And of course, who was I sat next to?

Clue:

Bald.

Beaming smile of welcome.

Same stained uniform as yesterday.

'Hiya,' Lizzie whispered. 'Guess what? We're going to hear *Isobel Gowdie* again.'

I still missed the quiet opening of *The Confession of Isobel Gowdie,* too busy seething at Lizzie. Bloody limpet, I glowered. How do I get shot of you once and for all?

And I wonder: Was *that* the moment when the notion slid into my head?

While I was too wound up to hear any melody whatsoever in *The Confession of Isobel Gowdie* second time around, and its pops and rattles and scrapes reflected the way I was feeling inside: Sour. Vindictive. Cruel.

And, weirdly – back in Merlock Park again.

Or was it later, when Jacko put all that *knowledge* at my fingertips? There for the taking . . .

'Impressions?'

Switching off the music, Jacko's eyes swept the class over his lopsided gregs.

'Speak to me,' he boomed, whirling his arms to generate some energy from six rows of sleepy weeds.

'Sir.'

Reliable Einstein Elaine was there. 'Pete and I think there's good struggling against evil.'

The Gerbils nodded keenly in agreement.

'Something horrible's happening.' Caroline's voice was barely a squeak.

'Definitely,' smiled Jacko, tactfully swinging attention away from Caroline before her burning cheeks set her hair smouldering. 'Anyone else like to share their thoughts? Nicola Nevin? You and your absent friends are usually bursting with verbiage.'

Before the summer I'd have blushed puce at being singled out and expected to think on my feet like this. I'd have stuttered out some limp offering so quietly that I'd be made to repeat what I'd said, cringing at the way it sounded even lamer the second time round. Yvonne and Caroline would have tried to comfort me with one of their *I know how you feel* looks.

However, since chumming with Isabella, I'd wised up, learning the value of a sullen shrug when teachers pick on you. You should try it some time, specially if the teacher's a softie.

Dunno, your shrug could mean. *Don't care.*

Most teachers, if they've any wit, move on before they're the ones left looking like spanners, waiting for an answer they're never going to get.

But, of course, Jacko Jackson, he was way too smart to care about looking stupid.

'Your thoughts, Nicola?' he pressed.

Thought it was clashing noisy junk, I was about to sigh just to get Jacko off my back. Well, it *was* an opinion. But before I could say anything, Lizzie had one hand up, the other sliding her notebook across my desk.

'Please, sir,' that confident voice piped up. Her elbow was digging at me. 'We made loads of notes in music. I'll read them, coz Nicky won't follow my writing.'

Follow your writing? I was thinking as Lizzie nudged me

reassuringly. Cleared her throat. What writing? When did these four pages of scrawl appear?

'We thought *Isobel Gowdie* was disturbing, and beautiful and sad,' she began, looking over to me every few words to suggest she was speaking for both of us.

'We imagined Isobel being picked on and tortured and then burned. The composer made his strings and percussion sound like . . . like real objects you'd use to hurt someone . . .'

And so Lizzie blabbered on. When I sneaked a glance round about to check what the rest of 4C made of all this industry from the bald one, half were flicking over their own notes, adding to them here and there. Jacko didn't stop anyone. Nor did he stop Lizzie mid-spiel with his own superior opinions. He stroked his chin until Lizzie finished up, 'The music was powerful enough to make us scared like Isobel must have felt. We really connected with it.'

'How *inter*esting. Thank you,' Jacko said, inspecting Lizzie over his glasses as though he was seeing her for the first time. 'I'm delighted you were *both* so moved,' he added, pursing his mouth doubtfully at me.

'And you were spot on to feel scared in Isobel

Gowdie's situation. She lived in an age of superstition and paranoia, one victim of the Great Scottish Witchhunt,' he said, chalking key words on the board. 'Right up until 1772, in fact, anyone, particularly any female who seemed *different*, was in real danger of becoming a scapegoat for misfortune in a small community. If cattle sickened, or children died, people looked for someone to blame, and accuse. You could be labelled a witch simply by being too old, too beautiful, too weird, a different religion. You might have healing powers that didn't always work or, more than likely, you were a stroppy bisom, prepared to stand up for yourself. They'd say a woman like that – fit for anyone, feisty – had *smeddum*. That is, until someone called in a witchhunter to teach her a lesson for being independent. Part of this joker's job was to poke at you with his brods, looking for the Devil's mark.'

Jacko, who relished any opportunity to inject a dod of panto damery into his lessons, was giving it one of his mimes now. Arms stretched long in front of him, he stabbed at the air close to my face as if he was playing virtual pin the tail on the donkey.

'Please, sir, what are brods?'

'What's the Devil's mark?' voices called out.

'Well, what am I doing?' asked Jacko, moving to the back of my chair, parrying between my shoulder blades now. 'What does it look as if I'm doing?'

'Poking her?' Einstein Elaine volunteered.

'*Pricking* her,' Jacko corrected, 'with my sharp metal brods. That's my job. Why am I doing that?'

'Coz she's a cow,' I heard someone – one of Peter Gibson's mates – mutter.

Lucky for him Jacko was too deep in character to bother. His fingers were hovering over the top of my head now.

'I'm searching her scalp. What am I looking for?'

'Wee cooties,' another of the boys called out, and I felt Lizzie bridle at my side. I'd a shiver down my neck from what Jacko was pretending to do. You know that way you bristle when someone's touch is close?

'*Come* on,' Jacko urged. 'Haven't you seen this in one of those ghasty horrors you watch when you could be reading? Duffy, or Sabina the Teenage Bitch?'

So sad, sir, groaned the silence. Then Lizzie put Jacko out of his misery.

'Sir,' she said. Quietly. Almost reluctantly. 'You're

looking for a spot where Nicky was meant to be kissed by Satan. She won't feel pain there, no matter how hard you stick the pins in. It'll give a witchhunter proof she's a witch.'

'Exactly.' Jacko quit his stupid mine. 'A wellspring of knowledge in a desert ignorance. My mummery was not in vain,' he flounced, wiping his brow with a weary sigh. 'Was there a film, or a story you read, Elizabeth?'

Now, I've wondered: Was it *here* that the notion that slid into my head in music took hold of me?

When Jacko left off pricking *me* for a witch in front of 4C?

When the real thing was sitting right beside me?

See, Lizzie hadn't watched any film about witchpricking.

'My gran's gran's gran's gran was burned as a witch,' she said.

15

MARGARET

SUN SIGN: ARIES ♈

RULING PLANET: MARS ♂

An Aries tends to be a poor judge of character.

Aries hate to be physically restricted . . .

Couldn't help feeling sorry for wee Nicky when she showed up at Bella's yet *again*. This time muggins here was sent down to chase her.

'Don't let her over the door, Mags,' Bella warned.

'Is that coz you don't want her seeing all that ointment on your face in case she tells Luke what a sight it looks?' I asked. Well, I was only stating the obvious. Pink gunk everywhere. Plukes poking through like fairy lights. Don't think Bella was too happy with my suggestion.

'Get lost! It's coz I can't be arsed with her.' She booted me downstairs. 'And if you let her in, Mags, you can let yourself out.'

Honestly, that Bella treats me like an unpaid bouncer sometimes.

'Hi, Nicky. Sorry. Isabella's not feeling up to seeing *anyone,*' I'd to shout over Guess Who belting out 'Toxic' on the karaoke machine upstairs.

Felt rotten, so I did. I mean, where was the harm in Nicky popping in? Might even have stopped Bella obsessing about her palooka joes for five whole minutes. Especially as Nicky was *bursting* to talk, words tripping over her train tracks soon as I opened the door. It was all a bit of a jumble:

'Mags, guess what?

Gotta tell Bella.

We're gonna write this essay for Jacko about witches.

Guess what?

Oh, you've got to let me in.

They burned Lizzie Brownie's gran as a *witch*.

Jacko says that means Lizzie's a witch's get.

That's born of a *witch*.

Lizzie'd've had to watch her step long ago.

People would suspect her of things.

Accuse her of stuff.

And guess what?

She knows *everything* about witches.

God, the more I think of her the weirder she is.

Let me tell Bella.

Puleeeze!

Lizzie sang this song in music and it gave everyone the willies.

Then she was *crying* when Mrs Jacko played this Scottish thing.

The Confession of Isobel Gowdie, it's called.

Isobel was a witch.

Just like Bella.

No, I don't mean Bella's a witch.

Getting mixed up.

Just the name.

Weird, innit?

Coincidence.

Isobel. Isabella.

And all these things happening.

Bella's skin.

It was fine till we went up to Merlock, wasn't it?

To that Drowning Pond.

Know what I'm thinking?

What if Lizzie Brownie's a real witch?

I mean, she'd all these notes but I never saw her writing.

What if she cursed us?

She's always muttering.

You'll be sorry she said that day I saw her nits.

And listen, this is the freakiest thing.

It's totally actually hideous.

Right.

Listen to this.

Jacko says witches have places where they feel nothing when you hurt them.

Well, guess what?

Right. See, at the end of English?

My bag caught between my desk and my chair.

So I shoved my desk away and it trapped Lizzie's finger . . .'

Poor Nicky. Don't think she took a breath while she was rabbiting. Her face was getting redder and redder. Eyes wider. Speech faster. Pitch higher . . .

Crank herself up any more and she'd have an eppy. Bella would *not* want that on her doorstep!

So I interrupted. Put my hands on her shoulders. '*Calm* down, *calm* down,' I said, like that plonker in the advert, pretty sure Bella would want to hear *some* of this. But then one of her stilettos flew downstairs and clonked the back of my head.

'Get rid of the Gerbil, Mags.'

'Sorry, Nicky,' I said, closing the door on her face while she was still talking.

'. . . trapped her spazzy finger.

'Ripped it away from her hand.

'It was pishing blood. But Lizzie said she didn't feel a thing.'

'Rancid,' was all Bella had to say about what Nicky had done to Lizzie when I gave her the gist of it. As she was inspecting her forehead through a magnifying glass at the time, I wouldn't swear she was paying any heed.

16

JUST AN ACCIDENT . . .

Luke was pinching my earlobe to illustrate his point.

'There can't have been nerves in the extra finger, Nick. That's why Lizzie wouldn't have felt anything. It'd have been like tearing this.'

Ouch!

We were both jostling for space in the kitchenette, me peeling spuds while Luke browned the mince. It was the sight of him chucking raw beef into a pot that set me confessing what I'd tried to tell Margaret.

'Lizzie *swore* she felt nothing. Blood everywhere, though,' I said, deciding to give mince a miss tonight.

'The poor girl,' Mum called through from the living room. 'Hope you apologised, Nicola?'

'Course,' I snapped, irritated that Mum would think I didn't have the wit to say sorry. More irritated that Mum's question rekindled the memory of my panic as I watched Lizzie's eyes goggling from my face to her finger, my face to her finger . . .

'Sorry, sorry. Just an accident . . .' I'd chanted uselessly till Peter Gibson elbowed me aside to staunch Lizzie's hand with his gym shirt.

'Who took her to hospital?' Mum was asking, bumping her chair round to the opening of the kitchenette. This story had fair perked her from her usual tea-time slump when she watched Luke and me, or Dad if he was here, doing all the cooking.

'Dunno,' I said. 'We left her with the nurse. They were trying to contact her foster home.'

'Och, poor girl. Foster home. You need to phone. See how she's doing. Why not ask her round? Make it up to her.'

That'll be right, I was thinking, wishing Luke hadn't opened the kitchenette door to let Mum hear our conversation. Now it was twenty questions.

'Lizzie's not a pal, Mum,' I told her, pushing back the wheelchair to set the table. 'Anyway, it was just an accident. Lizzie knew that.'

Watch yourself next time, Nicky, she'd said.

'That's *my* job, Nicola,' said Mum, snatching at the cutlery in my hands, but missing as her fingers closed in spasm before she could grab properly. 'And *I'd* like to know that girl's all right, accident or not. I can hardly run round to the school and ask, Nicola. So you invite this Lizzie here.'

I was snookered now. Mum would do this to me. Use her illness to . . . well, not to get one over, but to force my hand. Emotional blackmail, that's the right term, though I feel rotten even using it to describe Mum's behaviour when she's the way she is. But I mean, if Mum was – well – normal, and she said she wanted to meet the likes of Lizzie, I'd say, *No chance. That* freak. But how could I even *think* about saying that when my own mum's twitching in a chair, her speech gone funny, her legs gone dead? You just want to keep her happy.

'That'll be a bundle of laughs. You know Lizzie's the nitty one?' I explained to Luke over Mum's head.

His reaction floored me.

'That *babe* with the shaved hair?' Luke whistled. 'Amazing green eyes. *Nothing compares to you,*' he crooned as he crumbled an Oxo cube into his mince.

I couldn't believe we were talking about the same Lizzie here.

'Well, you can duet with her if she comes round,' I

snapped at Luke, and the next thing I was describing Lizzie's solo in the music lesson, hamming up the way she sang with her eyes closed and her chin poking out.

'How the heck can you think she's fit? She's a lollipop,' I told Luke. 'Said her gran's gran's gran's gran was a witch.'

'Wow! When do I get to meet her?' Luke replied, belting out his Nina Simone now. 'Maybe *she'll put a spell on me.*'

Luke had to bide his time. It was more than a week before Lizzie returned to school, showing late for Old Groat's Wednesday biology class. With Isabella of all people. This was *her* first day back since pond dipping.

'Where have you two been?' Groat rounded on them, chalky index fingers mustering them to a spot on the floor in front of her.

'Well?'

It was bizarre to see this unlikely pair stealing glances at each other to see who would speak up first. Isabella towering over Lizzie, seemed to be all hair. Metres of the stuff cascaded like a wavy curtain to her waist, covering her face in a style she'd never worn before. Lizzie, with her scrappy scalp, was the pale inverse of the scarlet-jumpered, pleated-skirted figure beside her, as washed-out looking as her should-have-been-white shirt. No wonder Isabella widened the gap between them with heel-swivels of her shiny shoes while Groat homed in on Lizzie.

'The nurse wanted to see my finger,' Lizzie explained. She waggled the dodgy dressing on her left hand.

'Of course.' Unbelievably, Groat's growl mellowed, though the glance she threw in my direction was as fierce as a hailstorm in June.

'You keep that clean,' she said, almost kind, nodding Lizzie to her seat. 'Now what's your excuse, madam?' she blasted Isabella. 'Lost your comb?'

Isabella, of course, had nothing to say for herself. Par for the course with most teachers. Dicing with death where Groat was concerned.

'Did the midges at Merlock eat away your tongue?' Groat demanded.

Silence.

A long, calculated silence.

Forcing a duo of sniggers from the back row where Margaret and Janet were lapping up every second of Isabella's defiance.

'Then SPEAK, girl,' Groat bellowed suddenly, making Caroline and Yvonne squeak. Her voice reverberated around the biology lab like a mini-earthquake, test tubes trembling in their stands. Anyone who wasn't quite with it this midweek morning was wide awake now, workbook open, pen poised. Isabella, however, remained mute, only shaking her head casually to restore the long strand of hair displaced by Groat's spittled yell. She stood tall, neck arched. Cool as cocktails.

'Groat's lost it,' Margaret's foghorn whisper informed Janet, loud enough in the bold silence Isabella had created for everyone to hear.

'You think so, Margaret?' Groat laughed humourlessly, while the rest of us winced in anticipation of what was coming next. 'Perhaps we can discuss what you mean during interval when you and Della Rosa are planning your detention schedule with me. In the meantime, I've a class to teach.' With these words Groat shooed Isabella to the side of the blackboard.

'Stand there, dear, and for goodness' sake tie that hair off your face. This is a laboratory, not an experimental salon.'

Isabella sashayed to the blackboard, hand on hip, and parked her left buttock on a bookshelf. Legs crossed, arms folded, her tongue poked through the smile playing behind her hair.

Groat soon straightened her out.

'Stand up,' Groat barked, taking a scrunchie from her drawer and thrusting it at Isabella. In the same heartbeat the lesson continued.

'Habitat of a freshwater pond, Elaine?' Groat snapped, only the psycho-killer with an Uzi threat in her voice hinting at the mood she was in.

Groat had planted her tweedy self in front of me to dictate notes, blocking out most of Isabella behind her. All I could see were two elbows wiggling like a pair of animated jug handles stuck to the side of Old Groat's head as Isabella footered with the scrunchie.

I was quite enjoying the illusion until Margaret cried out, 'My God, Bella! Your face!'

I reckon, in her own way, Groat was being cruel to be kind when she made Isabella face the wall for the remainder of biology. Or maybe she just figured that short of putting a bag over Isabella's face, it was the only way of getting any work done before someone barfed. The sight of Isabella's coupon exposed was not for the fainthearted.

* * *

It was the talk of the steamie after biology.

'Isabella's like the Elephant Man,' Rosie Meek, who was always fainting, said faintly. 'What's on her face?'

'Some kind of orange ointment,' suggested Einstein Elaine. Eleven out of ten for observation.

'It's caked on,' said Yvonne

'But all those bumps are poking through.' Rosie pressed her own smooth forehead.

'They're weeping,' Caroline shuddered.

'They're pustules,' Einstein Elaine nodded wisely. Trust her to know the correct technical term.

'They're squishing her eyes down,' Molly Mone added, dragging down her own eyelids as if any of us needed reminding

'All right. Show's over! Bella's dead sensitive. Bog off,' Janet interrupted protectively. She shooed the cluster of us down the corridor, then planted her girth in the width of Groat's door. Arms folded at her chest, legs splayed, she looked like a bouncer on duty. When I joined her, Janet shook her head.

'Not today, Nicky. A-list only,' she said, staring over my shoulder. 'Anyway, your pal's waiting.'

'Hey, Nicky.'

Right under Janet's nose, Lizzie Brownie bloody well shoved a scrap of paper in my hand. She was smiling. 'Luke said you wanted this.'

'Luke?'

There was a phone number scrawled on the paper in spider writing. Yug!

'Yeah. He introduced himself. Wow, he's *so* decent, Nicky,' Lizzie giggled. Leaned confidentially towards me. 'Says my hairstyle's awesome.'

Bloody Hell! No wonder Janet's lower jaw was moving south. This little exchange would get straight back to Isabella.

I power-walked Lizzie down the science corridor, feeling Janet's eyes boring my back. Wished I could just clamp my hand over Lizzie's big mouth so Janet wouldn't hear that clear voice landing me in it.

'I'd love to come round,' Lizzie was trilling. 'Any time. Just say when. Tell me now rather than phoning. No one gets their messages at my place. Oh, and my hand's fine, by the way. Luke said you were in a state about it.'

Before I could wheech her from the science corridor,

Lizzie held up her grubby dressing for me – and Janet – to admire. I recoiled, not so much at the dressing, but at the state of her shirt cuff. It was stained crimson. Can't have been washed since her accident.

'Is it gonna be all right?' I asked, my voice more sullen than interested.

She shrugged. 'They froze it. Cut off the finger. Stitched me up.'

'Good,' I said.

'Yeah, well . . .' Lizzie said. Her giggle had evaporated. She flexed her bandaged hand, lost in thought. 'Feels weird without it,' she said. 'My gran said all the women on her side had an extra finger. Brought them luck . . .'

Luck?

'Come on. It looked . . .' *Disgusting,* I nearly said, before I caught the expression on Lizzie's face. Faraway, she was, lips moving silently the way they had on that bus to Merlock.

'. . . looked like it could catch on things,' I garbled.

'Never bothered me. Never even bled before,' said Lizzie quietly. 'My gran told me that would be a sign –'

'A sign?' A shiver frizzed all over me at her words, round my shoulders, creeping up my neck to my scalp, tingling my spine, goose-pimpling the entire surface area of my skin.

'Someone wishes me harm,' Lizzie said, her green eyes puzzling mine before she broke my shiver with a laugh.

'Couldn't be you, though. Just an accident, and worse things can happen,' she said, the giggle back in her voice. 'I mean, the state of what's her name again . . . Isabella?' Lizzie frowned vaguely, clicking the fingers on her injured hand. Then she exhaled, fanning her face.

'Whoooo! What did she do to deserve *that* flare-up? Specially when her skin was so clear. Rather her than us, Nicky, eh?' Before I could dodge away, Lizzie was squeezing my arm. Just as Isabella, flanked by Janet and Margaret, rounded the corridor and witnessed the gesture.

17

TEA-TIME FOR A SHAPESHIFTER

'So what's the game with Lousy, Nevin? Holding handies now!' scowled Isabella.

'Just can't lose her, Bella,' I said.

We were both in the doorway to Jacko's room, me ignoring the wave Lizzie gave me from the front of the class. While Jacko clapped sharply for everyone to settle in their places, Lizzie pointed to the empty seat beside her with a smile.

'*Somebody loves ya, baby,*' sang Isabella, a push to the small of my back tripping me towards Lizzie. In an acid voice she added, 'By the way, Jan says Lousy's sniffin' round my Luka but *you're* having her to tea?'

Before I could explain that one, Jacko loomed over Isabella until she slumped in a chair at the back of the room and opened her English folder.

I didn't invite her, Isabella, I wanted to say. *It was my mum . . .*

That in itself was a tricky one.

Because way back in the summer I told Isabella my mum was too sick to entertain visitors, especially when Dad was on the rigs.

Why had I lied to Isabella? After all, before I quit being a Gerbil, I'd no problem whatsoever with Caroline and Yvonne being round Mum the way she was. It didn't seem to matter that she couldn't do anything for herself or that her speech sounded like someone putting on a spazzy voice for a laugh. Caroline and Yvonne never behaved any differently towards Mum. When there's an invalid in the house you notice things like that. Caroline and Yvonne didn't raise their voices like Mum was deaf as well as wheelchair bound, or – like her GP and nurse – speak v-e-r-y s-lo-w-l-y as if she was brain soft.

No, I have to say that Caroline and Yvonne were just themselves. Shy. Polite. Always asking Mum if they could have a drink, thanking her for having them to tea – which they'd cooked – blushing when she egged them on play her their latest kittens-being-strangled violin duet.

'Your mum's great,' Caroline and Yvonne would still

tell me, unembarrassed that she drooled and slurred.

I always suspected that Isabella's reaction would be a different kettle of fish altogether. It was obvious from the way she reacted to Luke telling her Mum was in a wheelchair that night they met in Capone's.

'O, povera madre,' she'd sighed into Luke's eyes, her own so wide that they brimmed with tears of compassion.

But then she'd swiftly changed the subject to describe her own mum's brand new car. Lovestruck Luke probably thought Isabella was being tactful that night. *I* knew though, even then, that she didn't want to know about Mum because disabled people and old people and fat people and ugly people revolted her. She slagged them openly. *Crips totally give me the heebie-jeebies.*

So how could I possibly invite her round to mine? I knew I'd be embarrassed by the expression on Isabella's face, ashamed that my new friend was repulsed by Mum twitching in a wheelchair. Ashamed of my once-pretty mum that is. And of course, I'd be even more ashamed of myself for being ashamed of my mum. Ach, it's complicated . . .

I know this because Isabella, sick of angling for an invite, had already turned up one night on spec in those weeks she was dating Luke.

'Surprise!' she'd said, kissing me on both cheeks when I answered the door. Breezing past me.

'Is my lovely Luka in? Show me your room, Nicky.'

Isabella was in our sitting room before I could warn Mum and Luke there was a visitor. She couldn't have picked a worse time. Mum was having her dessert, Luke spooning yogurt into her the way Mum spooned it into him once. They were playing the One for Mummy game. Made it easier to get through mealtimes since Mum started having problems swallowing. Luke was brilliant at it, making a joke out of a situation that wasn't one bit funny.

'One for Johnny Depp in the nude,' Luke was chanting. 'One for Bryan Ferry, kissing your toes.'

Mum was making yum noises whenever Luke named someone she liked, though judging by the look on Isabella's face it must have sounded like a gargoyle puking. Before Luke realised she was standing there he spiced up One for Mummy by sticking in a few of the usual folk who really made Mum gag.

'One for Victoria Beckham. One for the Queen with an invite to her garden party.'

This was the point in the game where Mum closed her mouth tight. She joked this was her payback for what Luke used to put her through when *she* fed him. He'd to force the spoon between Mum's lips until she laughed. This was seriously messy – I couldn't do it. Don't know how Luke could do it – but, just like Dad, he never seemed bothered.

'You clat,' Luke was kidding Mum as she spattered him, wiping both their faces with the same sticky cloth when I coughed politely.

'This is Isabella, Mum,' I said, cringing for all of us.

That look on Isabella's face, there was nothing like it with Lizzie Brownie when I finally invited her home on a night I knew Isabella was holed up in detention. I'd been dreading Lizzie's visit all the same, postponing it as long as possible.

It was heinous, folk from school seeing us sit together on the bus, Lizzie prattling on about how much better our school was than her last one. Me trying not to look at the bloodstained shirt Lizzie hadn't changed all week.

Did Mum notice Lizzie's unkemptness? I'm not sure. She was probably too taken aback by the other things that happened during Lizzie's visit.

'Hey, that's some hairdo,' Mum said when I brought Lizzie into the sitting room. She was holding her hand out to Lizzie. Just like on that evening when Isabella visited, it wouldn't keep still, jerking about like it was conducting some crazy, silent orchestra. I wondered if Lizzie would get what Mum was doing or would she, like Isabella turn away and make some inane comment about the wallpaper nearly matching the carpet?

'Hello, Mrs Nevin, I'm Lizzie,' said Lizzie, following Mum's dancing hand. Before it twitched away from her, she grasped it with her own damaged hand. Then she looked Mum straight in the eyes, something both Luke and I noticed Isabella had found impossible.

'I'm sorry, Mrs Nevin,' said Lizzie, 'I didn't catch what you said. What's the matter with you anyway?'

Well, that was different for a start, I thought, watching the gobsmacked look on Mum's face.

'Mum says she likes your hairdo and we don't know what's wrong,' I answered for Mum, swithering whether Lizzie's directness was tactless or refreshing. No one, to my knowledge, had questioned Mum's condition so openly before. Not Caroline, not Yvonne, not even the neighbours.

'Degenerative disease. Muscle wasting. Incurable,' Mum said. Recovering from Lizzie's questions she spoke slowly.

'Hey, I understood *that,* Mrs Nevin,' Lizzie beamed. 'Degenerative disease,' she repeated as slowly as Mum had pronounced it. 'That sucks,' she said, plonking herself down on the chair nearest Mum so they were eye level. 'Is it like MS?' she probed. Bloody hell, I thought, though there was something about the way Lizzie asked that didn't seem nosey.

Mum tried to shake her head.

'Different,' she said, adding quietly, 'Quicker.' She was staring down at herself as if her body didn't belong to her, that look I dreaded darkening her face like grey clouds.

Good for you, Lizzie, I thought. Two minutes in the door and you've put my mum on a downer. If something didn't take her out of herself quick she could be staring into space for days. Not talking, not eating. Worrying us all crazy. I was hopeless at dealing with Mum when she got like this, too upset myself to jolly her before her black dog slunk in like an uninvited guest. If Dad or Luke were here they'd work magic, whipping up rotten jokes from nowhere. Dad would whisk Mum off in the car: a concert, a film, birling her away from her dark cloud in a spiral of positive energy. But me? I just didn't have the knack, my own misery reflecting my mum's back to her, compounding it.

Can I make you a cuppa? That was the best and worst thing I could say. Pathetic.

'Tea?' I glowered at Lizzie, addressing Mum's turned away face, 'and hey, Mum, Luke'll be home soon. What kind of pizza d'you fancy?' I was babbling at the barrier of silence around Mum's chair. There was no response, Mum's hands twitching in her lap. Then Lizzie said, 'Have you ever tried massage, Mrs Nevin? I know you don't have MS but my gran used to treat people with it, and she taught me.'

The tone of Lizzie's voice turned Mum's attention to her. Gran was a kind of healer, Lizzie was saying, and before Mum knew what was happening, Lizzie had reached for Mum's hands and drawn them across to her own knees.

'She used oils to ease spasms. Might help yours, Mrs Nevin.' While she talked Lizzie was running her palms down the insides of my mum's cramped hands from wrist to fingertip in a constant rhythm. All the time she spoke, rapidly, softly, never pausing for a second. Her voice, I noticed, had a singsong pitch, almost as if she was chanting, and the more she spoke, the quieter she grew until only Mum could hear her.

'I could bring some oils next time,' was the last thing I made out before Lizzie's words were whispers.

Well, that took the biscuit!

'*Next time!*' I snorted beneath the affronted shriek of the kettle. Dream on! Lousy was lucky she was still here in one piece. So bloody forward! Asking Mum about her illness, then giving her a load of mince about oils and healing. *Nothing* would heal my mum. I'd put Lizzie right on that one! Soon as she stopped feeding her New Age pish and offering false hope I'd tell her. Then I'd chuck her out.

I splashed water in the teapot. Set out mugs. One for Mum. One for me. When Lizzie left I'd regale Mum with our guest's solo performance in Mrs Jackson's music lesson. I'd dig out my baldy man wig and I'd do Lizzie, singing up like a complete spanner. *Anything* to cheer Mum up . . .

Though Mum didn't sound upset. In fact, the choky sounds coming through from the sitting room were her laughing. Really laughing.

'What's so funny?' I snapped when I swung through the kitchenette door.

'Lizzie's telling me about shaving her hair off.' Mum's voice was bright as sunlight. 'Her foster mother started and the clippers broke, and she couldn't face scalping the rest with a razor, so Lizzie had to do it herself . . .'

'With a hand mirror, using my right hand,' Lizzie added, 'My head was cut to bits,' she told Mum, rubbing her hand from the nape of her neck upwards, rasping the bristle. 'I quite like it now, though. It's different.'

'I like it too,' Mum said, doing something I'd never noticed her do with anyone new before. She was slowing down her speech to let Lizzie pick up every word for herself, rather than letting me interpret. Then she did something else. Something that she never even did to me or Luke or Dad any more. She reached out a wobbly hand and squeezed Lizzie's arm.

'How's your finger?' she asked.

'Brand new.' Lizzie peeled back her scaffy plaster. There was a purplish dotted line running up the outside of her finger. 'Dissolving stitches,' said Lizzie, trying to restick the dressing. 'Itchy, that's all.'

'Lizzie, I'm really sorry for what Nicola did,' Mum said. Her arm vibrated on Lizzie's grubby sleeve. She was frowning into Lizzie's face. Looking sorry for her. My mum, in her state, feeling sorry for anyone!

'No big deal. Accident,' shrugged Lizzie, 'Right, Nicky?' she looked over her shoulder and grinned at me. Mum wouldn't have caught that briefest flare of accusation in her eyes. Blink, and I doubted I'd seen it myself.

'I should hope so, Nicola,' Mum raised her voice sternly.

'Course it was an accident, Mrs Nevin,' Lizzie said, 'and there was no need to ask me round because of it,' she added.

'But you're Nicola's friend,' Mum began, and I cringed. D'you think Lizzie's the best I can do?

I retreated to the kitchenette to rip open pizza boxes and clatter a few plates. Where was Luke? He'd forced this stupid tea party, flirting with Lizzie in school. Now he didn't bother showing up to help me out.

I'd tell him to butt out of my business, I thought, though when he did come in I could have hugged him.

* * *

Everything would be fine now, I smiled to myself, hearing him greet Lizzie warmly.

And I must say, I'd *never* have bargained on lousy Lizzie and my brother Luke hitting it off quite so famously. And I'm not talking about him being his usual chivalrous self. I'm talking about going overboard. Tumbling his wilkies. Head over heels. Looking at Lizzie like he wanted to *eat* her.

What I found particularly gross was how turned on Luke was by Lizzie's lucky finger.

He had to know *all* about it. Did it still hurt? Had she lost a lot of blood. Did Lizzie get to keep the amputated digit as a *souvenir*? (No, in case you're wondering, though I have my doubts!)

Lizzie and Luke's heads were close enough to catch nits from one another. Last time I'd seen Luke pay anyone this much attention, he'd been smoochied up to Isabella at Capone's. She'd explode if she saw this little scenario.

'What about anyone else in your family? Did they have this extra finger?' Luke asked Lizzie, cupping her hand in his.

'Well, my gran had it, and she said *her* gran had it.'

'Not your mum?'

'Dunno much about her. Always lived with Gran. Till she died last year.'

'Oh, Lizzie, I'm sorry, pet.'

To think I'd been worried about entertaining Lousy Lizzie Brownie. Honestly, I might as well have disappeared up my own backside in a singing ball of fire for all the notice Mum and Luke paid me the rest of the night.

They were hooked, two Nevins in thrall to Lizzie's green gaze.

This shouldn't be happening; a shilpit wee scadge like Lizzie hypnotising my mum with her presence, capturing my brother's heart. What's more, Lizzie seemed to be blossoming from the attention Luke and Mum were giving her, the sum of all her fairly unremarkable features changing from drab to unignorable like she was some kind of twenty-first-century shape-shifter.

Me? I was withering from neglect! At one point I put the telly on, just to see if Mum would pull me up for bad manners. She didn't. And I switched it off.

Listening in.

To every word.

18

LAVVY CHAT

Isabella, Janet and Margaret were crossing the yard, arms hooked together, when I caught up with them next morning.

'How was detention, Bella?' I asked, blaming Papa's wheelspin for the fact that she didn't reply.

'Love your hair, Bella,' I tried again, peeking round Margaret to catch Isabella's eye. 'Never seen you with a fringe before . . .'

Big Margaret cut me off with a rib-busting shunt, the fingers of her free hand dotting her forehead with pretendy spots.

'It's camouflaging the plukes,' she muttered out the corner of her mouth. Oops! Wasn't doing too well so far, was I?

'Guess what?' I tried again. 'Lousy Lizzie's lived in four different foster houses this year. Keeps on having to leave them.'

'Why? Is she too grotty?' sniffed Margaret. She didn't break stride; didn't look at me. Nor did Janet. She scratched her head as she walked.

'So crawly she gets moved on?' Janet let the door we'd reached swing into my face.

'No. She's on the adoption list now her gran's dead. Says no one'll take her at fifteen. She's an orphan –' I persisted until Margaret interrupted me with a loud yawn.

'Fascinating –'

'– The Story of Nicky's New Mate,' Janet yawned too, 'but not our mate. Eh, Bella?' she snorted.

I was trotting to keep up with the three of them now, spluttering my appeal to Isabella. 'Lizzie's not my mate. She's a freako. Into healing and stuff.' I smirked. 'Luke drove her home and the place she's living's this complete dump. Kids everywhere –'

'Luka took her home? Why?' Isabella's nails dug my arm.

Bingo!

'Luka took Lizzie home?' Isabella repeated. 'What else did Luka do?'

Isabella yanked me back before I reached the school hall. We were late for assembly now, Mrs Jackson at the piano, rippling the intro to 'Morning Has Broken'. Sneddon the Head Un scanning the stragglers.

'Hi, Nicky,' Lizzie whispered, hurrying past me. 'That was great last night. Your mum's brill. So's Luke. I've brought in the stuff he wanted. Give you it later . . .'

Lizzie was speaking over her shoulder to me, moving down the hall, taking a seat with the rest of 4C, but that was the last I saw of assembly because Isabella had me outside in the yard again, double-stepping me into the girls' lavvies.

'You can say I felt sick, Nevin,' Isabella said, peering into the graffiti-etched mirror above the washbasins. With the flat of one hand she pressed her new fringe to her forehead, the other groping in her schoolbag until she pulled out a pair of rechargeable hair straighteners.

'*Merda*!' she scowled. 'I am sick of *this*.'

I felt like a voyeur, watching while she ran a finger along her wavy fringe, lifting it into the ceramic clamp of her irons. Underneath the hair, that forehead of hers was livid with sores. Some crusty, some weeping, some scabbed over.

'What a pain, Bella,' I winced, praying I didn't sound patronising. She said nothing, though her scowl deepened beneath the cloud of hairspray she blattered at her fringe.

'Now, Nevin,' she said, fanning her chemical fallout my way. 'What's this about Luka and the *strega*?'

'The what?'

'*Strega*. That witch.'

Isabella's eyes slid to the mirror. As if she was thinking aloud, and I wasn't even there, she spoke into it.

'Why would Nicky invite Lizzie to her house when Isabella never gets invited? And why would Nicky introduce Lizzie to Luka when Nicky knows Isabella wants him back?'

Isabella pouted into the mirror. As her gaze narrowed I felt panic beat a pulse from my throat to my temples.

'Maybe Nicky just doesn't want to be Isabella's friend any more?' Isabella's words clouded the glass, making her reflection disappear. 'Maybe Nicky likes Lizzie better? Maybe Nicky wants Lizzie to be Luka's girl?'

'It's not like that, Bella,' I began at last. Then I gulped. See, there were names swirling about in my head:

> *Luke Lizzie Isabella Lizzie Nicky Lizzie Isabella Lizzie Luke Lizzie Strega . . .*

An idea surfacing.

Lizzie Strega Healing Stealing Spoiling Charming Lizzie Witch

Slowly, like an object I couldn't identify yet, my idea was floating on a pond of muddy water.

Lizzie. Strega. Witch.

It was taking shape, forming into something solid enough to placate Isabella.

'In fact, you know what I think about Lizzie, Bella? I think she's a w–' I began.

But the first period rang as I spoke, drilling apart my life-saving theory for now, jolting me back to reality.

'Oh shit,' I said, picking up my schoolbag. 'We're drafting our essays for assessment this period. We're late now.' I'm glad I didn't add what was running through my mind: that I needed a decent grade, that Mum would be really upset otherwise . . .

Because Isabella smiled. Pressed her hands to her face.

'*English,* Nevin? Oh my golly gosh! You'd better dash. Hurry to class like a good little Gerbil.'

And I *so* nearly turned back when she called across the yard after me, 'I'll get your gossip later, right, Nevin?'

19

CREATIVE CONSTIPATION

Of course I had to headbutt Sneddon on my way back into school, didn't I? Spent the next fifteen minutes on the threadbare patch of carpet in his office where all the reprobates scuffed their toes, precious essay time ticking away while he read me the riot act for being late.

And then some.

He was *delighted* I'd bumped into him, he drummed his fingernails on his desk and told me, not looking delighted at all. Just so happened he'd been wanting a word. Been watching me lately. Noticed a change, he said. Not for the better. I wasn't the focused young lady I'd been in lower school, was I? Members of staff were reporting I'd turned lippy. Work sloppy. Marks slipping. Not what he'd expect from Luke Nevin's sister. Eh? Eh? I'd changed my friends over the summer, hadn't I, Sneddon mused. Made me remind him who I hung around with now.

'Della Rosa, Muir, Pike,' he laughed dryly when I told

him, rippling his thumb through a bundle of files. 'Their referrals are never off my desk. Funny that,' he added grimly, taking a fresh folder from his drawer and writing my name on the cover.

Fifty lines he gave me: *All that glisters is not gold.* Put me on a behaviour card to be filled in by every teacher.

'Tardy,' Jacko wrote with a flourish in the first box. Before I could explain myself he directed me to the empty seat in the front row.

'You can see we're all working too hard to be disturbed by your feeble mendacity, Nicola. Forty-five minutes left,' he whispered so harshly that nearly every head in the class shot up. At the back of the room, Margaret and Janet grinned at me. I could hear Isabella's pen rattling against her smile when I took my place next to Lizzie Brownie.

Don't you dare speak to me. Things are bad enough, I glowered at her.

But Lizzie didn't even seem to have noticed my arrival. Not for a second did she stop writing, her left hand zig-zagging across her workbook faster than a turbo-charged laserjet printer. That skanky plaster, I noticed with a shiver, rubbed the paper and caught on it, but it didn't bother Lizzie like it bothered me. Head low, lips moving, she rattled through her essay. Page after page after page . . .

Me? Oh, jings! Don't ask. I'd creative constipation. Always the same writing essays. Really like doing it, but man, is it hard! Can never find the right words or tone when I need them. Even though somewhere in my head I know how I want everything to be in my story. I can picture it. I can *feel* it. Smell it. Touch it. Just can't write it.

At home I'd drafted a plan, trying to remember how freaked I'd felt hearing that *Isobel Gowdie* piece the Jackos had played. I decided I was going to retrace Isobel's death walk through the streets of her village. People would be lined up to mock and jeer. I'd detail their faces, leering, malevolent. Describe the way they jiggled in front of Isobel, taunting her to charm herself free. *Turn yourself into a crow and fly,* they'd mock. *Change into a black cat and sleek away. Ride off on your broomstick . . .*

I could really see these people mocking this poor woman. The rotten teeth in open mouths, their plaids and shawls, the babies in their arms. I caught the heat off them crowding the streets. I could smell their breath, their sweat, the straw at their feet, the smoke of their cooking fires and their livestock.

And then there was Isobel Gowdie herself, shuffling on bound feet, bruised and bloody from the torture she'd been through. Young, I pictured my Isobel. Small, skinny, filthy, shilpit, scalp all torn and bleeding where she'd been shaved and tortured.

She was shrinking from the mob as she was rope-led towards the pyre where she'd die. I wanted to show her twisting and writhing to escape, begging for her life. I wanted her voice to sound like the voice I heard in my head. It was singsong and distinctive.

'I'm not really a witch. Please spare my life,' she'd plead through bruised lips and smashed teeth. 'I'm innocent.'

Sounds good, eh? Well, don't get too excited.

If you had the misfortune to mark my dumb essay instead of Jacko you'd find it hard to believe I was capable of imagining all these things.

Soon as I tried to channel all these brimming thoughts from my head down the barrel of my pen, I stalled. Managed three pages of drivel, boring myself skelly with my own turgid storytelling before Jacko told us to stop writing. I handed in my workbook completely scunnered.

Maybe that was why, when I stood to leave, I bumped Lizzie so hard that her pen skited across the last page of her story. She'd still been writing, see. Longer than *War and Peace*, her essay.

'You've to finish,' I said.

'I have,' she smiled, rubbing both hands down her face. Left it smeary with black ink. 'Was that the bell? I was miles away there,' she said, eyes all bleary. '*Love* writing stories,' she said. 'Don't you?'

'You kidding?' I said, belting out of class before she could chum me. '*Love writing stories,*' I muttered to myself, not realising I was speaking aloud until I saw the nudges Yvonne and Caroline exchanged at my expense.

Great day so far, I glowered, storming up the corridor.

Stupid sarky Sneddon the Head Un, keeping me back from class on the one day that I didn't want to swan in late. *Drop dead, dipshit,* I mouthed at his window. And pompous old Jacko. I'd come in today keen to do my best and he'd refused to hear my excuses. No wonder my essay turned out pish. I could picture the disappointment on Mum's face already.

'Nicola! Why can't you just keep your head down like Luke?'

Luke. I was mad with him, too. This mess I was in so far, I realised, was basically his gorgeous fault.

If he'd kept his hormones to himself, hadn't had his summer fling with Isabella, I wouldn't be Sally Solo, watching Caroline and Yvonne nibble their health bars on the bench the three of us always used to nab. I'd still be sitting among them, perfectly content, discussing choir, and hoping we'd be netball subs at gym next period. If he'd taken his brave pill, Peter Gibson would wave hello. At some point during break, Isabella Della Rosa and Margaret and Janet might sashay past, arms cleeked, on their way to loiter outside the boys' bogs. None of them would think to throw us Gerbils a glance.

But it wouldn't matter. *I'd still be a Gerbil,* I muttered, wondering where I could go to take the bare look off myself, so people wouldn't think I was a sadcase who didn't fit in anywhere. Like *her.*

20

FLUSHING FALSE HOPE

You'd think Lizzie had a sixth sense. Soon as I glowered daggers into her back she swung from the noticeboard and ran towards me. All smiles despite my torn face.

'Nicky, for Luke,' her voice rang, loud enough to turn heads. She was stuffing all these papers in my hands. 'I'll just explain what these are . . .'

'Toilet,' I interrupted her.

Unusually, the bogs were empty. Knew it by the way my anger ricocheted back to me through the pungent silence. I leaned against a cubicle door, Lizzie's sheets clasped in one hand. They were covered in her spider scrawl, all these facts about oils and herbal teas. How their properties were meant to do you good.

Grated ginger for nausea.

Lavender for sleep.

Peppermint for stomach cramps.

Blend the following oils to relieve spasm, I read, before

shredding the sheets and flushing them down the toilet. *Toss the crap to kill false hope.* If Luke asked I'd say I must have dropped them.

Down the lavvy pan, and good riddance, I told the swirling scraps. None of Lizzie's remedies would make Mum better, would they? Or ease the pain of her knowing I was on a behaviour card. *What's wrong with you, Nicola? You used to be my good wee girl.*

When I thought of Mum's disappointment on top of everything else she'd to put up with, my anger evaporated, turning into something else that made me weak and sad. If I hadn't heard someone calling me over the howling cistern, I'd have howled myself.

'Nevin, you in there?'

At the sound of Isabella's voice, I brightened. She was looking for me.

'You got problems down under, girl?' she laughed, her friendly tone making me forget that all the crap I'd landed so far today hadn't really been Luke's fault, or Sneddon's or Jacko's, but hers. I even did my best to pull her up about it.

'Thanks a bundle for the hassle I'm in,' I ribbed her, any remaining anger lost in the translation. Instead my reproach creased her up.

'See, when Sneddon nabbed you, I sneaked past him,' Isabella hooted, tiptoeing round me. 'Then I told Jacko I missed assembly coz, *Please, sir, it's m'bad week, sir.'*

Isabella doubled over, groaning. 'Complain about your basement to a man and you get off with murder,' she advised. 'Speaking of men,' she went on, 'what's with crawly-head and my Luka?'

It was funny. I felt better. Isabella, Janet and Margaret were my pals again, huddled round me. Like in the Devil's Den whenever we'd something to discuss. Isabella had my arm, her fingers fiddling with the two friendship bracelets she'd given me.

'Spill the beans on Lousy,' Isabella whispered excitedly as Margaret gave my waist an encouraging squeeze.

So I did.

'I'm not kidding, you guys. Lizzie was a pure embarrassment. Eating things off the table before we were ready to sit down,' I lied, pretending to stuff my mouth with bread.

'You'd think she'd never seen food. Cleared us out of drinks an' all. *Is there any chance I could have some more juice, Nicky?'* I wheedled, secretly recalling how I'd poured the cola Lizzie barely touched down the sink once she'd left.

'And,' I told Isabella, not altogether sure how she'd take this, 'she was a wally with my mum. Pretending she understood her. *Hee hee, hee Mrs Nevin,'* I giggled, trying to block the picture of Lizzie stroking my mum's hands from my mind's eye.

'Bored the arse off us all with this hocus-pocus healing crap,' I scowled, grateful for the matching girns Janet and Margaret were wearing. *Tell us more,* their greedy eyes said.

'She went on about these stupid oils her granny taught –' I began, when Isabella drew her arm from mine.

'Who gives, Nevin?' she yawned. 'Thought you were gonna tell us about Lizzie and Luka getting *hot.'*

I could have lost it then. The threesome breaking the circle, abandoning me for their reflections as the bell rang. Isabella was scowling at her forehead again, fluffing her fringe over her craters while Janet and Margaret applied synchronised circles of lipgloss to their twin pouts.

'Better go, gals,' said Isabella, hand out for Margaret's lippy. I wasn't included in her summons.

So I piped up.

'Bella, Lizzie was *all* over Luke. Total slag. Offering to massage him. Told him her bloody life story too and missed the last bus deliberately so he'd to drive her home. I'm after flushing away all these leaflets she brought in for him.'

What was I like? Only the last thing I said was true. But I was desperate.

Can you see that?

A few porkies put me back on track with Isabella. Where was the harm?

'Go on, Nicky,' Isabella said, hooking her arm back into mine as we crossed the yard to gym.

21

GOOD SPORTS

The changing room was chock-a, ripe with 4C sweat by the time Isabella slung her kitbag towards the furthest corner of the benches.

'Why's that slut changing in my corner?' Isabella queried loudly when she spotted Lizzie.

If Lizzie heard, she didn't let on. She was working her heels into this pair of scadgy plimsolls. They had to be at least one size too small. Her greyish towelling sports socks bulged over the sides of the shoes like folds of elephant hide.

'Meant to wear green and gold socks in this school.'

'And white trainers,' simpered Janet and Margaret, unpacking their own pristine kit.

'Wee Jinky'll kill her,' hissed Isabella.

But Wee Jinky Johnstone, our poppet-sadist of a gym teacher, did nothing of the sort.

She'd bigger fish to fry.

'Oi,' she greeted her four latecomers. 'You dollies breezing in after the bell, never you mind gawping at me through forty layers of mascara. I know I'm gorgeous! Kits on and butts into my gym. MOVE IT!'

This was the Wee Jinky we knew and loathed. Four and a half feet of evil with a voice like Jimmy Krankie on helium. No one messed with her. Even Isabella changed without argument. That is, until Wee Jinky was no longer standing over her.

'Lezzy in a bottle! See her staring at my boobs?' Isabella sneered into her cleavage while Wee Jinky was worrying the rest of 4C into the gym.

'Five seconds, or else,' Jinky warned us, chinning an imaginary bar.

'Away you go,' said Isabella, though she made sure she'd her kit on first. While she waited for the rest of us, she swiped Lizzie's uniform from the bench to the floor, then booted everything about the changing room.

In the gym, Wee Jinky had 4C warming up with shuttle runs.

'Do fifty. Let's see you lay-deez SWEAT!' she bawled from her vantage point at the top of the horse.

Obediently Janet and Margaret galloped away like palominos, leaving Isabella and me to jog off together.

'Look, Bella, Wee Jinky's keeping up high so she doesn't get trampled under somebody's hoof,' I puffed at Isabella as we shuffled listlessly. My comment wasn't hellish witty, but for some reason it cracked Isabella up. She let out this shriek of mirth and stopped dead in the middle of the gym, her outstretched arms creating an obstacle that caused a sudden and major pile-up.

'What are you all *doing* down there on my floor?' Wee Jinky bellowed into tangle of legs and hair and brown gym pants below her. She bounced up and down on the horse, blowing her whistle at the same time. 'On your feet, 4C. Only one of you's still running.'

'Check that out!' Margaret, who was sprawled on her stomach, wheezed. She pointed towards the end of the gym where the solitary figure of Lizzie Brownie was plodding in her slip-slop plimsolls.

'Lo-*ser*,' singsonged Isabella.

'*Good* work, Elizabeth. *Keep* going,' Wee Jinky encouraged as Lizzie passed her, 'The rest of you jokers UP and RUN! Else you'll sprint till the end of the period, never mind how clammy it is!' growled Wee Jinky.

'Good work, Elizabeth. Would you look at that daft bint?' Isabella sneered. She waved a languid hand for me to hoist her upright, and together we jogged off, Margaret and Janet flanking us. Up ahead ran Lizzie.

'In a wibbly-wobbly world of her own,' I bitched. And I don't know why this happened but spontaneously the four of us were aping Lizzie Brownie. Clumsily we ran, on flat feet, legs splaying sideways from the knee down.

'Look at her all sweaty,' one of us said.

'Sadcase.'

'Slut.'

'Witch.'

I say one of us because, to this day, I'm not sure who said what. Isabella or myself. Honest, I don't know.

But I do know this: whoever said it, she was wrong.

Evil, as Luke reproached me when all this came to a head.

And I doubt either of us would have been so mean if we'd foreseen the consequences of our cruelty.

When Margaret stuck her foot out – *Watch this, guys!* – the clatter of Lizzie's fall made the wall bars vibrate. She fell too fast to save herself, knees, elbows, hands, chin scudding the deck *really* hard. I heard the hollow clack of tooth meeting tooth inside her jaw.

Lizzie didn't move at first. No one did. She sprawled, face down, while 4C played musical statues. Wee Jinky leapt off the horse like a *Kill Bill* assassin and skidded fast as a curling stone across the gym floor.

'Elizabeth, can you hear me?' Wee Jinky knuckled Lizzie's upper arm. 'Come on now. You're all right.'

Lizzie groaned, twitched her arm away and moved her head a fraction.

To the left of me, Isabella tutted.

'Shame. It lives.'

'What happened here?' Wee Jinky asked. She scanned everyone, her eyes narrowing on Isabella.

'How should *I* know?' Isabella sniffed, eyes wide. 'Musta tripped in those shoes.'

'Right enough,' said Janet, chewing on her thumbnail to hide a smirk.

'*Accident,*' fluttered Margaret. I saw her wink at Isabella.

'I'm OK.' Drawing up one leg, then the other, until she was crouched on all fours, arse poking north, Lizzie rose. She was cupping her bad hand to her chin. Blood dripped through her fingers. Puddled the floor.

'You've bitten your lip. Always feels worse than it is,' Wee Jinky told Lizzie lightly, though she spent ages dabbing Lizzie's injury where she'd fallen before she'd let Einstein Elaine take Lizzie's other arm and help her to a bench.

'Gross,' muttered Isabella, watching Wee Jinky gather up handfuls of bloody paper towels. 'The wee lezzie should be wearing surgical gloves,' she scowled. When Wee Jinky put her arm round Lizzie's shoulder and Lizzie giggled, Isabella rounded on Margaret.

'You boobed there, Mags. Lousy's fine. Jammy witch. She's even getting to sit out bloody netball,' Isabella grumbled while Wee Jinky doled out positions for the game we were finally going to play.

I stared at the figure slumped on the bench, a pile of tissues in her lap. There was blood all down Lizzie's yellow gym top, darkening from red to brown as it soaked in. *Ugh*! Her bottom lip was bright and shiny, turned inside out from swelling, jutting too far from her face. She kept dabbing at it, probing her wound with her tongue.

And behind that fat lip, Lizzie was talking to herself again. Exactly, I recalled, with a shudder that chilled me despite the swelter of the gym, like she'd done on the bus when we travelled to the Drowning Pond in Merlock Park.

Trance-like as an old woman telling her rosary, Lizzie muttered. Believe me, she looked well weird, rocking slightly and sliding her eyes from right to left beneath half-closed lids without moving her head.

'Wake up, Numpty Nevin. Two passes ballsed up now,' Wee Jinkie screamed in my ear.

I didn't even recall her whistle blowing the game on. I was way too fixed on Lizzie.

She's tracking someone, I decided, missing the easiest catch ever from Margaret, who'd intercepted Rosie Meek with one of her superhuman Xena Warrior Princess leaps to claim the ball for our team.

Nearly four feet Mags must have jumped before she crash-landed. Highest anyone ever saw her fly.

'OK, so you canny catch a ball, Nevin. At least get it back in play. It's under the bench beside Lizzie,' Wee Jinky shouted despairingly, just before Margaret fell.

''Scuse *me*,' I snapped in Lizzie's chanting face, when she didn't move her feet for me. I was so close to her I smelt the blood on her top, the foot-honk from her plimsolls. Heard the whisper behind her fat lip.

'You'll be sorry, Margaret Muir, You'll be sorry, Margaret Muir. You'll be sorry, Margaret Muir . . .'

'Your foot musta hit the ground at the wrong angle, Margaret,' Wee Jinky claimed while 4C crowded the second victim of double gym. This one was an ambulance job.

Janet disagreed with Wee Jinky, insisting that Mags had been jumping like that for years. She never, *ever* landed wrong on those big strong legs . . .

'Sure you don't, Mags?' Janet asked, kneeling over her pal.

Margaret shook her head. It was an effort for her to speak. 'One minute I'm fine, then all the power drained from muscles. Foot just went,' she groaned. Her face was clammy. Green with shock.

'Don't try to talk,' Wee Jinky told her and shooed the rest of us off to get changed. Lizzie, I noticed, stayed where she was on the bench and was first to leave the gym.

22

ISABELLA

SUN SIGN: LEO ♌

Lucky stone: ruby

Leos are natural leaders.

They love attention . . .

Poor old Mags, eh? Every girl in 4C musta seen her cellulite, not to mention her overgrown bikini line when she was lying on the floor thighs akimbo. *Madre de Dio*, I'd've died of shame in the ambulance!

How come some females can just let themselves go like that? It's totally actually hideous. Mags, mind you, had a bit of an excuse. With her ankle bone poking out her skin she'd more to worry her than needing a Brazilian. But that Lizzie was well out of order back in the changing room.

I walk in and I'm greeted by her baggy wee arse poking up at me. She's scrabbling under the benches on hands and knees trying to regroup all the bits and bobs of her trailer-trash uniform.

'Oh, show some dignity,' I say, thinking, when I turn away, that it's Janet tapping my shoulder. But, hey ho, it's Nevin, and she's pulling this face that's uglier than Lizzie's backside.

'Guess what?' Nevin whispers in this really creepiod voice, nodding at the rear end reversing towards us.

'What?' I say, more bugged about how Lizzie could stand up and not *NOTICE* that her gym skirt was bunched over the top of her pants than any of Nevin's bibble-babble.

'*She'd* something to do with Margaret's foot,' Nevin says.

What crap, I'm thinking. Lousy wasn't even *playing* when Mags fell! I blank Nevin, *way, way* more bothered that Lousy Lizzie'd decided to squeeze herself in between the pair of us to change.

'There's no room here. We're here,' I put her straight.

Then wait till you hear the cheek of this!

'I changed here earlier,' Lizzie mutters.

'Sorry?' I says. 'You talking to *me*?'

Now, believe it or not, coz I'm no tough nut, but for some reason I've got clout in this school. When I tell someone to move, they move, and no one argues. But here I am, mouth open ready to ask Lizzie if she wants two busted eyes to match her lip, when she interrupts with a smile that shows dried blood staining all her teeth.

'I'm glad you're sorry,' she says. 'And I'm sure you didn't really mean to chuck my stuff around.' She's got the nerve to turn her back on me then. 'You won't do it again, either,' I swear she murmurs though she's pulling off her rancid T-shirt. And humming. Making the same sort of white noise I do during maths to wind up Lisa Marie.

Get her! Honest, I couldn't speak. Just gawped at Nevin like she was gawping at me. The pair of us reeled *totally* backwards when Lizzie stripped off. *Madre de Dio*! Talk about dirty bombs! It was like being sprayed by a skunk. Lizzie *reeked* of sweat and wore this *definitely*-not-meant-to-be-grey, saggy-cupped bra, one strap attached by a safety pin. If you think *that* was totally actually hideous, wait till I tell you that between Lizzie's shoulder blades there sprawled a dirty great birthmark. Looked like some kind of splatted insect – a winged beetle, or even a bat.

'Emergency. *Deodorant,* anyone?' I just *had* to shout and fan the air before I fainted down dead. And I'm sorry if it made everyone in the changing room stare at Lizzie. But she was *toxic.*

God bless Janet and her body spray for coming to the rescue.

'Let me skoosh this, Bella.' Janet zig-zagged her can across Lizzie's back the way you'd douse a fly whose card was marked. 'Irrestible Charm it's called,' she says spraying and spraying at Lizzie, even though she was shrinking away from Janet's aim. Drawing her arms so tight to her chest that her birthmark stretched across her back. Looked like a bat in flight now. Totally, actually *HI-DE-OUS*!

'D'you mind? Aerosols make me vomit,' said Lizzie, shielding her face from Janet's non-stop scooshing.

'Ditto BO,' I says, nodding for Jan and her can to keep doing a Major Service to Humanity. Until the spray coughs. Jams.

'Crap,' says Janet, shaking the can to her ear. 'There's loads left. Haven't used it myself yet, and it's right sticky. I'll be honking next period.'

I sent Janet to rinse out the cap. By the time she was back from the bogs Lizzie, like most of 4C, had changed and gone.

'What a scadge that lassie is,' says Janet, zipping up her skirt.

'D' you clock that mole on her back?' says I. And then

Nevin comes away with something totally unhinged.

'That's a witch's mark,' she blurts, her mouth tight and her eyes wandering all over the changing room like special voices in her head are telling her what to say next. Because what comes out is cuckoo.

'I heard Lizzie muttering just before Mags fell. *You'll be sorry, Margaret Muir.* That's what she said, Bella. That's what she said. I think she was putting a spell on her.'

Honest to God! What some folk do for a bit of love and attention!

'Never mind what Lousy *said*!' I'd to divert Nicky before she started dribbling. 'D'you check the state of her undies? Imagine my Luka groping *that*?'

'Haggard,' says Janet. But guess what? *She* was acting a bit weird an' all, examining her school shirt for ages before she put it on. Holding it at arm's length by the shoulders. Frowning. Her mouth was downturned. Looking like she'd just slugged sour milk with floaters.

'This isn't my shirt,' she says, sniffing the oxters.

23

SITTING OUT THE STORM

Poor Jan was stuck with Lizzie's shirt and there was no time to do a swapsie. We were already late for English.

'But I'm itchy. This shirt's scadgy,' moaned Janet, tugging at her collar like it was choking her while we hurried from the gym to the main school building.

'Never mind you, *carissima*. I'm getting wet here,' pealed Isabella. She stretched her hands up to catch the first pelts of rain from a louring sky.

I *thought* I'd heard distant rumbles of thunder when Margaret was being stretchered into an ambulance beneath steely, swollen clouds. Now a storm was upon us. I could tell by the thickness of the air and the prickle of sweat along my hairline, uncooled by the first hot splatters of a mighty downpour.

'You might as well have Mags' seat, Nicky,' Isabella shrugged as I held Jacko's door open for her. When she spoke, lightning forked across her face. Its flash was immediately followed by a manic tattoo of rain on the windows, as if a million fingers had been lying in wait outside, poised to rap for refuge when the storm began.

'The tardy trio, bringing the weather with them. I should take it as a portent,' intoned Jacko, gown billowing behind him as he swept us into the class. His words were accompanied by a long belly-rumble of thunder.

'Let me guess your excuse. *Please, sir. We were waving off the ambulance, sir,*' Jacko gushed like Isabella in grovel-mode as he flicked on the class lights. Eight fluorescent tubes buzzed and stuttered. Their effect, if anything, made the storm's gloom more intense. One of those days when the weather's dark mood toyed with us all like a prowling beast.

Anxious, it made me feel. I've never liked storms. They've spooked me so much I've seen me curled up, a whimper on Mum's lap, counting the intervals between each lightening bolt and thunder clap until I could get to ten.

'That's it passing over now, pet,' Mum would say, stroking my hair, and I'd picture this Fee Fi Fo Fum giant lurching across the sky out of sight. He's gone, I'd think, although the rain'd need to ease to a whisper before I'd relax.

Feels like something horrible's gonna happen, I thought, following Jacko as he weaved round the desks.

And I was right.

Because Jacko was flourishing our marked Isobel Gowdie essays, giving them a public appraisal.

'Elaine McCartney. Good solid writing as usual.'

Isabella nudged me and rolled her eyes, '*Che surpriso*!'

'A-minus,' I muttered back, aping Einstein Elaine as she simpered, flashing her workbook so everyone caught a decko at her grade.

'Yvonne, there's an action hero inside you bursting to get out. Your Isobel fancies herself as Joan of Arc. We'd a rebel army hiding over a hill ready to free the poor girl,' Jacko explained to the class. Yvonne slid down her chair in mortification.

'It was a ripping good read,' said Jacko, beckoning Yvonne to sit up again.

'But Caroline, yours was an *homage* to *Blair Witch*. So much panic going on that you forgot all about punctuation. Redraft, please.'

I heard Caroline's sigh all the way from the front of the class to the back. 'Quite a few like that,' Jacko frowned, casting around the classroom like a panto villain. 'Not bothering your ginger to spell or paragraph or use direct speech in the panic of being burned at the stake. What's wrong with you text-message spawn? Get your priorities right.'

Sheepish laughter was silenced beneath a massive crack of thunder. At least Jacko was in one of his *funny*-sarcastic moods.

'Peter Gibson,' he continued, '*your* Isobel was a cyclops with bad botox who dug up a baby's bones and ground them into powder . . .' grimaced Jacko.

'But, sir, witches did that. Stole babies . . .' protested Peter.

'Aye, but rubber catsuits weren't the new black in the seventeenth century. Nor –' Jacko was edging along our row now, waggling two workbooks, 'did they speak in *like gross* American jargon!

'In fact, here's a fascinating spot of twenty-first-century witchcraft, 4C,' Jacko said, two workbooks cracking louder than the thunder on Isabella and Janet's desks.

'Two lassies and between them they come up with the

same repeat of *Buffy* that was on the box the night before they wrote this essay. Invent, don't recycle,' Jacko glared from Isabella to Janet, shaking his head.

'Now, who's still waiting for their masterpieces?' he continued.

A spattering of hands rose. Lizzie was one of them. As she tracked Jacko, she caught my eye. Smiled. I ignored her.

'Molly Mone. Sadly your splendid story was spoiled by a surfeit of sibilant sounds. Easy on the alliteration,' said Jacko. The next essay was mine.

'Workmanlike, Nicky,' said Jacko, with a shrug. 'Ain't what you say but the way that you say it. Ideas are good. Have another go.'

B-minus. I traced the red ink with my finger. Satisfactory. Average. Story of my life.

'Swot,' Isabella hissed at me, grabbing my workbook and sliding in on to her desk. 'Me and Jan got Fs. You'll need to rewrite our stupid essays.'

'Can't. I've to do my own –' I began to protest, as the biggest flash of lightning yet set the lights strobing. Everyone gasped, even Jacko. He'd been dusting his hands the way he always did when he'd finished with something. Now he raised them in the air.

'Blow, winds and crack your
cheeks; rage, blow.
You cataracts and hurricanes, spout
Till you have drench'd our steeples,
drown'd the cocks'

he shouted, shaking his fists at the window. 'Nature conspires to my purpose,' he declaimed, his voice all posh and trembly like a Shakespearean ac*tor* in one of his Friday treat videos.

'Looney tunes,' I heard Janet mutter beside me, the fingers of one hand working her shirt-collar. It whiffed of Lizzie when Janet raised her arm to twirl her temple with her finger and lean across me to grin – or was it grimace? – at Isabella. I closed my eyes. I was counting. *Six*, I'd reached. Thunder was passing, though the rain hadn't eased any. When I opened my eyes Lizzie's hand was up and Jacko was at his own desk, taking something from his briefcase.

'Sir, I didn't get my essay –' Lizzie was trying to tell him.

'I didn't get my essay,' echoed Isabella.

'If it stinks like you do *I* wouldn't want it back,' muttered Janet, wriggling in her chair.

Four rows away – and this is weird. You have to admit this is well weird! – Lizzie turned. Without lowering her hand. Her eyes, wide, unblinking, very green, seemed to bore into the three of us at once, her lips running away with themselves.

Mutter. Mutter. Mutter.

'Elizabeth?' said Jacko. 'Looking for this?' he smiled, though he didn't hand the workbook over.

'When I told you to imagine you were Isobel Gowdie, 4C,' Jacko said, 'I meant you to get under her skin, walk in her shoes. Elizabeth managed this with –' Jacko plucked the air for the appropriate superlative, '– *consummate* aplomb.' Retreating from Lizzie with a bow and a flourish, he signalled for her to stand and face the class.

'If you wouldn't mind indulging us, Miss Gowdie, we entreat you to deliver your final monologue.'

'*Madre de Dio,*' Isabella whumphed her folded arms hard on her desk.

'Gie's a break,' grumbled Janet, sourly. 'Feelin' crappy enough,' she burped, fidgeting loudly in her chair.

'Wheesht you two and learn something about getting

into character when you write,' Jacko warned. Sweeping to the back of the class, he perched on Isabella's desk like a raven on sentry duty.

'Soon as you're ready, Elizabeth,' he called as Lizzie turned and faced the class.

'I can't see who's saying these things about me, but I ken all your voices –' she began, taking a big breath. Her voice was weak and quavery and cracked and old. A whisper in the rain. In fact it wasn't Lizzie voice at all. Nothing like the clear, husky way she usually spoke.

'Canny hear you, loser,' Isabella sing-songed flatly. Yawning, she picked away at her old nail varnish.

'Rain's too noisy,' added Janet, groaning slightly. She was clutching her stomach, both arms wrapped tightly round her stomach.

'Speak up, Lizzie. Start again,' said Jacko.

24

ISOBEL GOWDIE'S FINAL JOURNEY

I can't see who's saying these things about me, but I ken your voices.

'Die, witch. Burn in hell.'

How could your gossip come to this?

'Mother Gowdie killed the laird's son. She sickened the minister. She lay with the De'il . . .'

Me? Aye, that's what you said, my neighbours. Tittle-tattling about me by the burn, in the lanes and fields. Now you're out lining the streets, here to watch me roast, though I've lived quiet among you, keeping myself to myself. Aye, unless you needed me.

'Can you help me, Mother Gowdie? You're a good sowl.'

Suddenly you've all changed your tune and you're pelting me with things I canny see. Stones. Dung. Sticks you've sharpened. Bones your dogs have chewed. Your bairns are dancing round the cart I'm tied to, shoogling the sides so my legs bang against each other. God willing I'll die from pain of it before I'm werrit. You all ken fine the Boot crushed my ankles in the jail, and if you dinna ken you only have to look at the state of me. But not one of you comes forward to tell their bairns to give a body peace in her last hour. You let them jeer me instead:

'You're gonny die you're gonny burn you're gonny die you're gonny burn you're gonny die you're gonny burn . . .'

Old Mother Gowdie cast a spell
Flew with the de'il
Now she's going to hell.

Some of you wee bairns wouldn't even be here if it wasn't for me. I birthed you, telling your faithers to make themselves useful instead o' standing there gawking. I made them wear your mammy's shift to draw the pangs from her own belly into theirs while she was labouring to bring you forth into the world. No one was keeping away from me then. No one was crying me witch.

'God bless you, Mother Gowdie. You've a gift.'

Plenty other bairns I've nursed from fever, their mammies banging on my door in the night.

'I canny wake him, Mother Gowdie. He's limp. His eyes are rollin'. In the name of God, help him.'

Did I refuse one sowl? Ever? Turn anyone away when you needed me? Och, you might have heard me grumble, or tell a lad who teased me to drop dead, but I never held his deeds agin him. Always did my best. Gathered water from a south-running stream and bathed bairns till they cooled, singing in the old tongue to wheesht them. Night on night sometimes I've tended an ailing bairn, drawing an infusion of herbs to feed drip by drop until a fever breaks. '*In God's name save him, Mother Gowdie,*' mammies have begged me. '*Use any power you've got. Just don't let my bairn die. You're an angel, Mother Gowdie. God bless your sowl.*'

Mother Gowdie steals bairns' bones
Goes to the graveyard all alone
Digs them up to make a pie
Eat a slice you'll surely die.

God bless your sowl . . . I'm heart-sick of hearing folk say that. Judge, minister, Witch Pricker . . . All these righteous men who think they're seeing justice done the day. Holy fools the lot of them.

My eyes are that bad I can't make them out but I ken they're all here. I smell their hypocrisy. Men wi' long black robes to match their long pious faces. They're following my cart, telling their prayers against the fife and the drumbeats thundering the air on every side of me. Wouldn't be right for these fine men to be seen joining in the jigging. They have to make sure everyone notes the Guid Book in their hands – after all, that's what gied them the right to take an aul woman to the fire. If anyone disputes their judgement they can say, 'We're only obeying Exodus: Chapter twelve, Verse eleven. *Thou shalt not suffer a witch to live.* And the woman on that cart is a witch and no mistake.'

Did she no' confess? We have her dittay in writing. Took a while, right enough. Thought she was going to die before we had the truth out her. But in the end, she confessed.

Isobel Gowdie bears the devil's mark
See her wandering the woods at dark.

If she lays bad meat down at your door
Your crops will die and your skin turn sore.

They had me strip. Fetched in George Scobie. Same wee snivelling excuse of a man who came to me years ago when he'd no means of making an honest living. Begging me to teach him love magic because he fancied setting himself up as a matchmaker.

I chased him.

Now he was trading as a Witch Pricker he'd forgotten how I'd set him straight before I shooed him off my land.

I knew nothing of magic, I told him then.

I know nothing of magic, I told him when he pricked me.

Scobie could only recall me laughing and muttering at him. Incantations that brought him out in boils, he swore in court. Liar, he was. Cruel with it, for he pricked me deep *all* over wi' his brods. Places on a body no man had the right to reach in an aul woman. Couldn't say whether I turned numb from shock or shame or cold, but parts of me couldn't feel anything by the time Scobie was done.

'God bless your sowl, woman,' he said like he was ordained Minister of the cloth an' all when his last brod

pierced 'tween my shoulders to the tip and I didn't cry out.

'Isobel Gowdie has a black mole there. Looks like a bat. I've seen that afore in other witches,' *Scobie told the court. 'It's where the De'il's kissed her.'*

In jail they pulled out the few teeth I kept in my head. Splintered my thumbs in the pilniewinks, drew my nails out one by one then flayed me. Big men, holding me down. '*Dirty aul witch,*' they called me. '*Nicnevin. Devil's hoor.*' I dinnae ken what was worse, the humiliation or the pain, made harder by the three days and three nights without sleep, without sup, when my jailers watched me till I couldn't think straight. Little wonder I told them anything they wanted to hear in the end. Someone was aye prodding me, slapping me, forcing water down me, questioning:

'Who do you worship, Isobel Gowdie? What spells have you cast?'

Different voices, Lord knows how many. One man would keep me standing naked to shame me to confession. When he left with nothing his relief bade me wear a shift dowsed in vinegar to nip all the scabs and sores ower my body. Next fellow bade the jailer shave my heed, then he tied rapes round my skull and twisted them tighter than a miser's purse-strings.

How I coped with this torture, I dinnae ken, but in all that time I said not a word. Whispered my prayers to shut away the pain.

Until the last man came. Left me with warm water for bathing, a clean shift. Ale to drink and bread to sup. Waited outside the door till I was decent. Then put his arm around my shoulders.

'*Who do you worship, Isobel Gowdie? You tell me now and be done with this,*' he said, his mien promising that anything I admitted would be our secret.

'*Tell me all about swinging a bag of boiled toads and nail parings ower the Minister's bed. Tell me about the waxen poppet you used to kill the laird's boy. Tell me about your Sabbaths in the woods with the Devil. Dancin' naked . . .*'

In my silence this man took a knife and scored me across the brow. Felt like a caress.

'*There now. Let us break this spell,' he said. 'Let us end this malefice. Then you can be free. God will take you back.*'

This man, he gave me his fine coat to wear and spoke kind.

I think he was the De'il himself, for his false promises made me betray myself.

'I worship Satan, sir. I do,' I told him, blood from my brow running into my tears. 'And yes, I am a witch. Now in the name of God will you let a body sleep.'

> *Isobel Gowdie weaves magic thread.*
> *She makes wax poppets and melts you dead.*
> *Isobel Gowdie has the evil eye.*
> *Danced with the Devil, now she's going to die*

To hear the clamour of this crowd now my cart's stopped, you'd think the fair was in town. There are fifes shrieking their mischief and drums rattling faster than my heartbeat. Bairns cry out, crushed, as men and women jostle close to take a right good eyeful. I can smell these people. Porridge and ale, sweat and excitement.

'Can she see us?'

'Dinna be looking in her eyes, she's chantin'.'

'She's black and blue.'

'She's shakin.'

'Dinna let the bairns too near.'

'Isobel Gowdie!' a Minister shouts in my lug but I hardly hear him over a roar that swells through the crowd like gathering thunder when a rough cloth is thrown over my head and I'm pulled down from the cart.

'Isobel Gowdie.' The minister's voice pipes thinner than the fifes drowning his words. I am a heap at his feet.

'You have confessed to flying like straw to meet the Devil, where you drank and supped in wild gorrovage, then lay with him. Under oath you have sworn he made you his servant and gave you sundry powers to charm by witchcraft and sorcery and that you did use these powers to curse Elspeth McLean and kill her husband John –'

Pater noster, qui es in coelis,

Sanctificetur nomen tuum . . .

While I'm praying they lift me. Two men taking an elbow, another jerking the rope binding my hands. They're rough, letting my broken feet drag and catch on the sharps sticks and branches of the pyre I'll burn on. When they stop they have to hold me upright for I canny stand.

'May God forgive your malefice,' says the Minister. Through the sack on my head I feel his thumb making the sign of the cross on my brow.

En ego, o bone et dulcissime Jesu, ante conspectum tuum genibus me provolvo . . .

Behold, O kind and most sweet Jesus, I cast myself upon my knees in Your sight.

'Don't waste your time on that Popish witch,' shouts Elspeth McLean when she hears me pray. Upon my shoulders something rests heavy for a moment before I feel it slip to my neck and tighten. A noose. Beneath the hood on my face my breath catches. It is time.

De profundis clamavi ad te, Domine: Domine exaudi vocem meam.

'Be done with her!'

'Light the fire!'

'Burn her alive!'

Scattered voices in the crowd jeer, though these are quickly wheesht by a silence that moves like the breath of God all around me. For a moment there is no sound save the whisper of my own prayers: *Out of the depths I cry unto Thee, my Lord.*

Then my noose is yanked once, lifting my feet off the ground. The crowd gasps so loud I canny hear the thoughts bursting in my head any more.

'*Dominus vobiscum.* The Lord be with you, Isobel Gowdie.'

All you did was stick up for yourself, telling Elspeth McLean she'd be sorry for refusing you a drop of milk. That's how it started. Wee show of smeddum from a crabbit aul woman. You meant nothing by it. Was just your way, for you'd helped her often and now she'd hurt you with her meanness. She kent and you kent her John didn't die that night because you shot him with elven-arrows that Satan lent you. Might even have lived if you'd tended his fever in time.

For that was all the power you ever had. All you've been good for: healing. That's how you ate, too blind and lame to work the land. God bless your sowl, Isobel Gowdie. A fool to yourself, you lied to make them stop and in these times not one person who begged help from you took your side for fear of being accused of malefice themselves.

All you've ever done is ease bokes, calm skins and break fevers with your oils and veneficiums. But who'll stand up for an aul crone who walked the woods at night talking to herself for company, gathering roots and herbs? Who's going to admit Mother Gowdie wasn't exhuming the corpses of unbaptised bairns for sorcery when they saw her digging earth in the churchyard, but tending her mother's grave. You saw me, Meg Pirrie, Janet McLean. You know I was praying in Latin, not summoning Satan with my incantations.

Will you stop this?

Will you tell them?

You were only gossiping because you didn't like the look of me.

If anyone's coming forth to speak for me they must make haste before I'm werrit. This noose has choked my speaking and my tongue has swelled to silence the truth.

Tell them.

They are hoisting me high, my legs dangling in air I can't breathe in.

It was only gossip of women.

Save me.

My head is hard against the gibbet. In one second they'll let go my life. I am dizzy.

Anyone?

No one?

Then I curse you with my last breath.

Isobel from the gibbet swinging
'Neath her hood you hear her singing
'I'm no witch,' she cries aloud
And leaves her curse upon the crowd.

25

DICED CARROT SURPRISE!

There was silence when Lizzie stopped speaking. Complete silence, for during her story the storm had passed, taking the rain with it. It would be brightening up outside, the air freshening, a tonic after the earlier swelter of the day. There'd be that lovely new-washed smell in the air, a peek of blue in the sky, reflected glint of sun off the puddles. Maybe even a rainbow. But here in Jacko's class, it felt like the mood of the storm had loitered behind itself in the huff.

Opening my eyes, I watched Jacko pull a long draw of air through his nostrils. His bones cracked as he moved away.

'Creep,' hissed Isabella when he was just and no more out of earshot, though she didn't mean Jacko. When I followed her gaze she was scowling in Lizzie's direction. 'Check that voice? *Exorcist* stuff. D'it give you the creeps an' all, Jan?'

Absently I glanced at Janet. Still felt, in my head, as if I was miles away. No. Years, centuries away. Standing . . . well, to be honest I saw myself standing among a guilty crowd. On *Gallow Hill* of all crazy places. Listening to a broken old woman. That thin, high voice Lizzie had used made every hair on my arm and neck prickle. And my focus was bleary. Or distorted. When I looked towards Lizzie, even the shape of her – just for an instant – seemed unfamiliar. Shrunken. Back hunched. Misshapen. Her hair grey wisps.

Lack of fresh air turning me doolally, I told myself. Seemed like I wasn't the only one affected by the stuffiness in the room either. In the seat beside me, Big Janet was looking none too clever.

Or sounding it.

'Crap,' she bellowed out the blue.

At least, that's what I think she said, because she was leaping to her feet as she spoke. Like someone had pronged her butt with a brod.

'Crap,' she repeated, louder this time, cupping both hands to her mouth as if she'd been afflicted by sudden Tourette's. Using her netballer's thighs, she oomphed her desk to the floor, straddling Isabella as she shoved along our row.

'Janet Pike, what is the meaning . . .?'

Immediately Jacko was flapping his way towards us, every head in the class turning to follow.

Except one, that is.

Up the front.

Although it wasn't till later on I remembered that *significant* detail.

You see, in the foreground of everything, there was just Janet, ignoring Jacko, changing direction and thrashing her way over my legs now.

And then I sussed why Janet was in such a hurry. Well, it became obvious when her final *'Crap'* heaved from the sump of her belly and erupted all over my head and face and uniform.

God knows what Janet had been scoffing lately; I avoided analysing the contents of her stomach once I'd identified the main life-form inhabiting the rockpool of vomit on my lap as diced carrots – there's a surprise – but Isabella swore there was *everything* in the gunk Janet sicked up. *Everything.*

This fact was verified by Einstein Elaine and Isabella. Since I was too webbed in orange spew to help Janet myself, Jacko dragooned the pair of them to hurtle their hurling classmate to the nurse. Twenty minutes later Janet's helpers joined me in the PE showers to sluice down, where they described in – frankly unnecessary – detail the six further projectile vomit stops they witnessed on the journey to the medical room.

'First there was this black stuff, Nicky. Right outside Jacko's door. Like an oil slick . . .' began Isabella.

'Or worms in treacle,' enthused Elaine, trying to interest me in a trace of something shiny on her skirt.

'Then Jan barfed up all this white milky liquid,' interrupted Isabella. She flapped her hand across her nose. 'Man, the ming off it!'

'And next there was a hairball,' said Elaine. 'I thought Janet would choke.'

Helpfully, Isabella gagged a re-enaction with a possessed Kurt Cobain rasping in the back of her throat.

'Hairball didn't smell, but –' she sniffed.

'Sort of blew away . . .' agreed Elaine, looking pensively into the changing rooms beyond. 'Like tumbleweed.'

She shuddered, stepping into the shower and giving me an unrequested swatch at the tumbleweed of her oxters *au natural*. All three of us were naked by now though for the one and only time in the history of all the school showers I'd taken, none of us seemed self-conscious, hiding our imperfect boobs or bums or bellies from each other.

Like me, I suppose, Isabella and Elaine just wanted all that puke washed away, the stench of it out our nostrils.

Although there was no end to Janet's vomit yet.

'After the hairball up came a lump of stuff like an owl pellet,' Elaine shuddered.

'Toenails jagging out,' Isabella added, winding her hair in one of the towels Wee Jinky had left in the changing room. 'Janet couldn't stand up straight any more. We were dragging her, teachers coming out to see what the noise was about. Should have seen Poofter Paige's coupon,' grinned Isabella, clapping both hands to her cheeks in camp horror. 'He *gagged* and squealed when Janet brought up a load of bile at his feet. *Omigod!*'

'At least Miss Groat wasn't squeamish. Drove Janet to hospital herself coz she said you never ignore someone vomiting blood.' Elaine was drying herself now, quickly. Sychronising her watch with the bell when it rang.

'Maths,' she gasped, picking clothes at random from the hotpotch of lost property Wee Jinky had provided so we could wear something unspewed-on home. Not even looking at what she was putting on, Elaine shoogled herself into a pair of brown nylon trackie bottoms that made her legs look like reject sausages in the wrong size of skin.

'See you. Hope Janet's all right,' she said, out the changing room before I'd the chance to tell her she'd Wee Jinky's Barbie towel on her head.

'Yeah, Nicky. Final barf. Blood.' Isabella's eyes were wide. 'Pure horror flick.'

'Wonder what caused it?' I asked, but Isabella didn't bother answering me. She was picking through Wee Jinky's jumble with the tip of a finger and thumb like there was something in there that could jump up and bite.

From the look on her face as she examined a Westlife T-shirt with beige sweat-rings under the arms I could tell she was recovering from the drama of the afternoon. Putting things back in perspective.

'Can't wear this cack. Does Wee Jinky think I'm a tramp?' Shoving her own sick-splattered tights into the pile of clothes before I'd a chance to pick something out for myself to wear, Isabella just about covered her decency with her towel, leaving her black bra straps on show. She kicked her blouse under the benches for the cleaners to find and used the Westlife T-shirt to wipe her shoes clean, soles included, throwing it back into the pile when she was done.

'No way are we sitting in Lisa Marie's class like fashion crimes, Nicky. I'm away to tell the office we're sick too. Papa'll pick us up. Need to get up the hospital to see Mags anyway.'

Left alone in the changing room it didn't take much effort for me to pretend to feel sick. Although I was showered and scoured, the smell of vomit clung to me. I kept seeing Janet draped round Elaine and Bella's necks, the dead weight of her straining the seams of Lizzie Brownie's washed-out shirt.

Lizzie Brownie . . .

NOW I recalled her head not turning when everyone else spun to check out the racket was Janet was making.

I remembered the set of Lizzie's back lost in Janet's big clean shirt.

I had an image of Lizzie's mouth. Muttering. Always muttering. Before something bad happened.

Silent words on the bus to Merlock . . .

In the gym . . .

In Jacko's class. After Janet and Isobella slagged her too far out of earshot for Lizzie to have heard . . .

And *that* was the moment when it happened.

'There's something unnatural about Lizzie Brownie.' My words hissed through the empty changing room. The chill of them made me gasp, and whirl around to see who had spoken. But there was only me. Nondescript Nicky Nevin. My fingers pressed to my lips.

I gulped, shaken at my own thoughts as I picked through Wee Jinky's junk.

Yet I just couldn't stop pondering that it didn't seem *right* for a girl the same age as me to possess all that insider knowledge about being a witch. And there'd definitely been more than a creepoid method-acting performance in Lizzie's reading of her Isobel Gowdie story.

'Bit of a coincidence,' I said to Isabella.

'Huh?'

Isabella wasn't listening. Blazer slung over her shoulders like a spotty Sophia Loren, she was waiting for Papa outside the school entrance.

'Bonus,' Isabella smirked when she realised we could look right in at 4C slogging away at maths. Whenever Lisa

Marie turned to squiggle another equation on the board, Isabella opened her towel and flashed her black bra.

'Check these statisitics, sir: 36B,' Isabella cooed, shimmying to make her boobs shoogle, although she'd have been as well setting fire to my farts for all the attention Lisa Marie paid her as he played with his numbers. She'd the desired effect on the male pupils in his set, however. A dozen mouths were hung open, wider than the rolling clown heads you chuck balls in at the fair.

Only the guy nearest us wasn't gawping. Peter Gibson was more interested in helping his neighbour. Gazing into Lizzie's green eyes, he pointed out the working in his jotter for her to copy down.

'Definitely a coincidence,' I said, louder this time. Blanking Peter's neighbour when she gave me a little wiggle finger-wave. Mouthing something that might well have been *See you later*.

'*She* hexed Janet and Margaret,' I suggested.

Carefully.

Slowly.

'Lousy Lizzie. Witch.'

A flush rushed my face when the words were out, and I shivered at the sensation, nausea surging in my throat, my scalp contracting beneath my wet hair.

What a mean accusation, a Luke-ish voice inside my head reproached me.

I could feel the smarm on my cheeks, anticipating Isabella's reaction.

If only she'd been arsed to listen.

'*Dio grazie,* Papa!' Isabella whooped. She didn't turn round once the whole journey from school to my place. Gabbed in Italian. Didn't translate anything, and I only convinced myself I was bodily in the car because Papa kept swivelling round on the approach to crucial road junctions to wink at me.

'I'm away up the hospital,' Isabella said when Papa swerved into the kerb at my place.

'Ciao, Nicky,' he kissed my hand wetly. Isabella didn't turn round.

'I'll . . . I'll come too?' My voice was unsure, seeking permission. When I opened the car door my uniform spilled on to the pavement.

'Not if you're dressed like a satsuma,' Isabella muttered in a couldn't-care-less voice, adding, 'I'm not *that* desperate to get back with lovely Luka.'

26
SCRUBBING UP

'Only me,' I called as I let myself in.

'You're early, love.' There was pleasure mixed with anxiety in Mum's voice. I heard her chair bump every item of furniture in the sittingroom as she manoeuvred herself to reach me. Her clumsiness set my teeth on edge.

'Wee accident. Hang on,' I called. I was thinking how Mum would enjoy the story of Janet puking on me. How she'd laugh at the state of me in an orange shell suit.

'Got your sunnies on, Mum?' I joked, pausing to check myself out in our long hall mirror. That wiped my smile away! What a puke I was myself, hair lank and slimy, eyes bruised with runaway mascara. I suppose I should also own up to my totally actually hideous caramel-chewing bahooky and thighs in those shell suit joggies. Looked like I'd stretched orange cling-film over them, the fabric strained so snug across the swell of my buttocks you'd produce a high note it if you bopped my arse-crack with a drumstick.

No wonder even the Gerbils were casting me pitying looks while Isabella flashed her tits at the boys, and Peter Gibson preferred his tatty little neighbour in her stale hand-me-down uniform to a psychedelic citrus fruit . . . with a personal hygiene issue of her own. The bundled clothes in my arms reeked of vomit. Vomit I'd have to clean off myself, I realised.

Isabella's mum would have *her* uniform in the bin already but my mum couldn't be allowed anywhere near mine. Couldn't risk her catching a bug. Last time she came down with something she needed a tube in her stomach to feed her.

So, instead of presenting myself to Mum, I locked myself in the bathroom, turning the shower, and Dad's radio, on full blast so I couldn't be accused of lying when I yelled, 'Can't hear you,' in reply to Mum's jerky scratchings on the door.

I knew my behaviour was mean, that Mum didn't deserve it, but just as there was nothing I could do about her illness, the special hoist over the bath, the adapted toilet seat we all had to use . . . there was nothing Mum could do about me locking her out.

I liked that.

Gave me a feeling of power strong enough to let me sluice my uniform out without the stink of it bothering me too much. When it was stacked up in a soggy pile on mum's bath seat ready for the washing machine I showered until there was no more hot water, soaping up with palmfuls of Mum's best Chanel wash. Felt better after that.

'*You are byoo-tiful, no matter what they say,*' I duetted with Christina, serenading the girl watching me behind the steam-skimmed mirror. While her hair was off her face I made her up carefully, plundering the make-up box under the sink that Mum never used any more. I winged eyeliner along the line of Mirror Girl's top lashes and stroked her eyelids with this smoky shadow Mum had bought for its name before she got sick. Purple Haze it was called, after some song Mum once embarrassed me by singing aloud as we stood at the checkout queue at Boots. It had never been out its box. Neither had Black Cherry Spell, the plummy lipstick I used to create Mirror Girl's pout. She looked five years older now. Gothy and dangerous.

'See you, gorgeous,' she winked through three coats of Lush-Lash mascara before I catwalked from the bathroom in a haze of the perfume Luke bought Mum last birthday.

'Hey, is Sicky-Nicky home?' I heard Luke's voice in the hall as I loaded my uniform into the washing machine.

'In here. Kitchen,' I owned up, convinced, even before Luke saw my face, that I'd overdone the slap.

'I hear people only need to look at you and they're barfing.'

Since I was bent double over the washing machine, Luke booted me playfully in the backside.

'Or was it something you said?' he said, adding, in a louder voice, 'Was it something she said, Lizzie?'

'Is Nicky all right?' that distinctive voice rang from the sitting room. Then it went on, 'Hiya, Mrs Nevin. Good to see you again.'

'Lovely to see you too, Lizzie,' I heard Mum greet her visitor, all cheery-cheery. Then her tone changed.

'Of course Nicola hasn't told *me* anything yet, Lizzie.' Mum sounded peeved, her voice growing louder as she wheeled herself to the kitchen doorway. I couldn't stay bent like an old hag over the washing machine any longer.

'Whoa!' gulped Luke, veering back when he saw my face.

'Were you painted up like *that* in school? No wonder you're home early,' snapped Mum.

There were three faces frowning at me: Luke recoiling with bemusement at my new look, Mum beeling, Lizzie all concern. They were waiting for explanations, but before they had any from me, I'd a few questions of my own.

'What you doing here?' was for Lizzie, not posed in my warmest tones.

'Why'd she come home with you?' was fired at Luke.

'Did you know about this?' That was for Mum.

Luke's explanation seemed simple enough although I don't think he needed to cross the room and hook his arm round Lizzie's waist before he gave it.

'We met up after school,' he grinned. Right into her eyes. 'She said you'd left early. Told me what happened in Jacko's. Tell you about that in a minute, Mum,' Luke promised, barely glancing from Lizzie's face. 'Lizzie thought you might be sick too, Nicky. So I told her to come back and ask her yourself, stay for tea . . .'

'. . . and I said yeah coz I wondered what you made of

those notes I gave Nicky to take home for you, Mrs Nevin,' good old Lousy chipped in. She was rummaging in this tatty hand-knitted bag. Glass clinked dully against glass inside it.

'I've brought my massage oils,' she said to Mum. Then she turned to me, 'and if you *are* queasy, Nicky, I'll blend some fennel and juniper. Do you a rub.'

'Hey! Can you do *me* a rub?'

Unbelievable! St Luke was being as suggestive as a Chippendale at a hen night.

Mind you, Mum didn't seem bothered. I suppose you stop sensing those kind of vibes when you're forty-plus. Or maybe Mum didn't care what was going on because she was too busy glaring me squirmy.

'I didn't get any notes, Nicola,' Mum said.

'I gave you them in school,' Lizzie tried to jog my memory. Oh, how helpful of her!

'I'd like to like to read them now.' Mum's voice was ice, her tone enough to send me out of the room. 'Wash that muck off your face while you're at it,' she snapped after me.

As I dressed I could hear the burble of chat from the sitting room and I wondered why conversations involving me and Mum never sounded so comfortable any more. Luke was reporting what he'd heard on the school tom-toms about Janet's illness, Mum gasping and chuckling by turns. Lizzie's voice only chipped in occasionally. She didn't seem to have much to say on the matter.

You'd doubt she'd even been there when it happened.

The pipettes holding her stupid oils tinkled different notes to accompany the conversation as they chinked against the neck of their bottles. Smells were wafting though the flat. Floral, musky, spicy, sweet. Mum sounded happy. Un-irritated. Relaxed.

Stuff this, I decided.

Time to do something about Lousy Lizzie Brownie before she worked a changeling situation on my family and substituted herself for me.

Yeah, time to teach her a lesson.

I kept my make-up on after all, reapplying more plum to my lips and smudging on a thicker layer of eyeliner.

I struggled into the black baggies Isabella christened Magic Kecks because she said they made me look thinner than anything else I wore. Matched them with my black lacy top. Its sleeves had special holes that looped over my thumbs.

'Found those notes yet?' Mum asked when I put my head round the door. The edge had left her voice and both her hands were unfurled, fingers loose in Lizzie's palm. The cosy little tableau was completed by Luke. He'd pulled a chair up close to Lizzie, his chin totally actually hideously *resting* on Lizzie's shoulder.

'I'll do the notes again, Mrs N. Don't worry, Nicky,' Lousy Lizzie smiled calmly, not looking up from Mum's hands.

'Don't worry. I won't worry,' I replied under my breath. 'I'm going out.' I spoke more loudly than I needed to, banging the door on Mum when she called me back.

'Out where? What about Lizzie, Nicola?'

'What d'you care anyway and what *about* Lizzie?' I muttered. Did Mum think I was hanging round to play second fiddle and entertain that *witch*? No chance.

Especially when I had all the goss I needed up my lacy sleeve to keep Isabella and the others interested in yours truly.

27

MARGARET

SUN SIGN: ARIES ♈

Lucky gemstones: Ruby or bloodstone,

which denotes courage.

Physical characteristics: Strong, big-boned,

energetic, athletic . . .

Poor Jan. Isabella nudged her so hard when Nicky walked into the ward that she fell out of her bed. Just missed my stookie, ending up on all fours, arse mooning through her paper gown. Not a pretty sight. In any normal situation Bella'd've shot a verbal rocket up Jan's bum crack. But all her attention was elsewhere.

'Hey, Jan. Mags. The sick-kids' clown's here.'

Bella settled herself more comfortably on Janet's bed. She clapped her hands like an excited kiddy but she certainly wasn't smiling and her eyes were narrowed, scanning Nicky up and down, up and down. No wonder.

I'd never seen Nicky wear so much warpaint. Certainly wasn't subtle. But it sorta worked. Suited the gear Nicky was wearing. Gave her an edgy, kinda *dangerous* look. I could tell Bella didn't like that.

'Some Gothy guy taking you blood-sucking, Nevin?' Bella sneered, 'Coz you're tarted up like a Bride of Satan. In't she, Jan? Oi, what you doing down there?'

Only now did Bella notice Jan trying to stand. Right away she snapped at Nevin, 'Gonna get Jan a seat? She's on a bloody drip,' and her eyes were all over Nicky's face, hair, gear, watching her settle poor Janet into a chair beside me.

'How're *you* doing, Mags?' Nicky asked, pointing at my plastered ankle, but before I could tell her that I'd cracked a bone and it hurt like stink and I wouldn't be playing netball for months, Isabella . . . Well, she sort of exploded.

'Duh! What's it look like, Nevin? They're both screwed. Mags can't walk and Jan can't eat. And what about me? I bought this out my own dosh. Twelve quid.' Isabella scowled from Nicky to the fruit basket on her lap like everything was Nicky's fault. Then she plucked a grape and fired it at Janet's head.

'Sorry, Bella,' said Janet. 'I'm having tests. Just in

case,' She explained to Nicky, almost too wiped to speak.

'In case what?'

'Case all that barfing was more than our Janet being a gannet,' Bella snorted.

'Bummer,' Nicky sighed, about to say something else when Bella really lost it with her.

'*Bummer*, Nevin? Is that all you can say? Check the three of us: her bones, her belly, my skin. And here you swan in, looking . . .'

Oh man, I wouldn't have been in Nicky's shoes for a place on the National Netball Squad when Bella kissed her fingers at Nicky. There was a twisted compliment lurking behind Isabella's black, hard stare, but there was no grace in it. Just dislike, resentment, boredom . . .

No wonder Nicky'd the same look on her face as my wee nephew when he's filling his Pampers.

Specially as Bella was just warming up.

'D'you know what I'm actually thinking, Nevin, seeing you here? Ever since you started hanging round, things have been going . . .' Bella's voice was light, almost playful, till she lifted a pear from the fruit basket and twirled it by the stalk.

'I mean Luke still ain't lookin' my way. You ain't doin'

me no good, girlfriend. In fact you could say we're all sick . . .'

Bella was smiling into Nicky's face. Teeth bared. Eyes hooded.

Poor Nicky. It was pathetic to see the way she took everything Bella dished out. There she was, smiling . . . no . . . *simpering* in this whinnying voice while her wee lacy arms gave it grovel, grovel, grovel as they reached out towards Isabella.

'Please, Bella. What you on about, Bella?'

Pure desperate, Nicky was. You could tell. From the way she was looking from me to Jan to Bella I reckon she'd have done *anything* to keep in with us.

That *sort of* explains why so much weird weird *weird* stuff came tumbling out her purple mouth. Nasty it was. All this paranoid crap about Lousy Lizzie.

'Hey, listen, you guys. I've been trying to tell you: this bad stuff's got nothing to do with me. It's Lizzie Brownie. She's a real witch and she's cursing us. Bet *she* made you sick, Janet. You made fun of her after gym so she passed something through her shirt. She's a witch's get, right? And she's into healing magic: oils and potions. She's cottoned on to my mum. Rubbing an egg over her hands right now at my place. Luke brought her home –'

'Luka did what?'

I don't think Bella paid heed to one word of Nicky's codswallop, more interested in spitting grape seeds into Jan's cardboard barfy-hat. Till Luke was mentioned, that is.

Then Bella wanted to hear all the goss on Luke and Lousy Lizzie. But not the Lizzie witch pish which was clearly an insane brain talking. It was only the girl-steals-boy business Bella was interested in. And in between Nicky's make-your-hair-stand-on-end cornflakes about curses and spells, she bitched herself a stay of execution.

'I'm not kidding, Bella, Lizzie's arse was on Luke's knee when I left them. She was offering to give him a rub-down if he took his shirt off,' I heard her telling Bella. The two of them left the ward arm in arm, Bella hanging on to every word Nicky muttered, Nicky hanging on to Bella for dear life. Between you and me and Jan and my stookie the pair of them looked well unhinged.

'Lousy Lizzie's finished,' Bella seethed as Nicky squeezed her hand in bliss. 'That witch is getting it!'

28

HUBBLE BUBBLE . . .

Oh yeah. Lizzie was getting it. There was no going back now. I'd to keep going. Persuade Isabella, Janet and Margaret that swimming Lizzie Brownie up Merlock was The Right Thing to Do. Can you see why? D'you understand how close I'd come to being outcast?

Anyway, what happened to Lizzie in the end wasn't just my fault. I'm sure there was Fate involved, because all this *witchenalia* was suddenly there when I needed it as Hallowe'en approached.

It had crept into my life with the visit to the Drowning Pond, continuing with that weird *Isobel Gowdie* piece in music, then the essay for Jacko put all sort of notions in my head. Felt like I was being shuffled into position to play my part in a drama I didn't create.

In fact, I *literally* played my part in a drama. Act 4, Scene 1 in Macbeth, as a matter of fact. Can you believe it? Out of all the zillion billion plays to choose from, Mr Bogle, aka Snot, our tragedy of a drama teacher, picked *that* one for our surprise assessment in Applied Performance Skills.

'You must call *Macbeth* the Scottish Play,' Snot was already droning to 4C as me and the others swanned in late to his studio one day in early October, 'especially if you're acting in it.'

Which we were.

And going first.

Now there's bad luck!

Snot only allowed us ten minutes to read through our lines.

'Hey, we're witches,' said Janet, flicking through the text.

'Whole stupid play's about witches, innit? *Hubble bubble toilet trouble.* You know all about that, eh, Jan?' Margaret's plaster nudged Isabella for approval.

'Piss off,' hissed Isabella. 'It's "toil and trouble", not toilet trouble, ya gimp.' She was studying our scene, counting up lines of text.

'Right. First witch has the most so say, so that's me. Second's you, Janet, third's Margaret. Nevin, you're Macbeth. His bits are all crap.'

My performance that day *was* crap. Stuttery. Stilted. Snot said he was disappointed. I'd been so convincing when I played Portia to Peter Gibson's Antonio in *The Merchant of Venice* last year. I was disappointed too. Six months ago I'd been able to follow the rhythm of Shakespeare's language no sweat when I rehearsed with Caroline and Yvonne. Now Macbeth's lines made no sense, so my performance was flat. I was a dull foil to Isabella, who made a . . . let's just say *memorable* first witch, delivering all her lines at least three octaves higher than her normal pitch. I kid you not. My ears are still ringing.

'Round about the cauldron go; In the poisoned entrails throw,' she screeched for starters in a Freddie Mercury falsetto, bearing down on Snot with an athletic stride that any wicked old woman would envy and a sneer that would curdle water.

While Snot and the rest of Isabella's audience clamped their hands to their ears, Margaret and Janet feebly intoned their *Hubble bubble toilet troubles*, as distracted as their audience by the spectacle of Isabella mounting Peter Gibson's desk, skirt hoiked over her thighs. When Isabella threw her arms aloft she seemed oblivious to that fact that Peter's head was up her skirt, and that everyone except her fellow witches, Macbeth and a boggle-eyed Snot was in convulsions.

'Speak, ya wally!' she prompted her Second Witch, staying in character when Janet failed to deliver her lines. By the time Janet had found her place, Isabella had nicked her part too, deploying an even shriller voice than the First Witch.

'Fillet of a fenny snake, In the cauldron boil and bake,' she glowered at Janet. Margaret didn't even bother attempting to read her bit. She managed to galumph about the stage on her bad leg when Isabella gave her the nod, and monotoned the *Hubble bubble* choruses with Janet, but basically Isabella played all three witches at once, whirling round the drama room with cackle and abandon.

'But why stands Macbeth thus amazedly?' she scowled, circling me in a witchy Christina-like dance at the close of the scene. Collectively, 4C wept silent tears of mirth.

'What a spirited performance, Isabella!' said Snot, initiating a shell-shocked round of applause, 'although I have to say you drowned out your fellow witches. Poor Macbeth's too dumbstruck to murder anyone. Let's see if our second group are more subtle.'

Guess who took centre stage next?

* * *

Lizzie, Yvonne and Caroline weaved through the drama room, carrying their schoolbags. They were chatting amongst themselves.

'It's raw tonight,' said Lizzie, rubbing her hands together.

'I've made lentil broth for after,' said Caroline. 'Warm us up.'

'Lovely,' said Yvonne. 'Let's get on then.'

The threesome knelt in a circle, not on the stage, but in front of it. Each emptied her bag methodically of its contents.

'Where'd you find the dog's tongue?' said Lizzie, turning Yvonne's ruler over in her hands.

'Cut it from Mary Weem's yappy Yorkie. Mind she wouldn't loan me a handful o' barley?' Yvonne sniggered, taking a pencil from Caroline and sniffing it gingerly. 'You found the bairn's finger, then?' she said. 'It's well rotten.'

'All the better,' said Lizzie. She closed her eyes and spread her hands over the objects ranged before her. 'Ready?' she asked, drawing a weary breath as if she needed to muster reserves of energy to do what she was about to do.

'Thrice the brindled cat hath mewed,' she began, delivering the first line of her scene in her normal voice. Clear. Slightly sing-song as if her First Witch was going through the motions of a task she could perform without thinking.

'Thrice and once the hedge-pig whined.' followed Yvonne.

'Harpier cries; 'tis time, 'tis time,' concluded Caroline, her raised voice the most actressy of the group.

Taking their lead from Lizzie, Caroline and Yvonne played their witches like ordinary women doing a job. As each took turns to drop an item into her imaginary cauldron, the other two watched with the respect of one professional chef for another. An approving nod passed between the First and Second Witch when the Third crumbled an imaginary birth-strangled babe's finger into the brew, her action reminding me of Luke adding an OXO cube to his mince. All three shared a job-well-done smile of satisfaction when Snot, appearing at Lizzie's shoulder as an Apparition, delivered his first line on cue:

'Macbeth! Macbeth! Macbeth! Beware Macduff.'

Now, I'm no expert at anything, as you know, but even I could tell there was something impressively *authentic* about this performance.

'They didn't seem to act, they seemed to *be,*' said Molly Mone to a murmur of agreement when Snot asked our class for comments.

'Made casting spells seem normal,' added Peter Gibson.

'That was brave,' nodded Snot. 'Who came up with the idea of acting like you weren't acting, girls?' He turned auomatically to Einstein Elaine.

'Lizzie's idea,' Elaine admitted, reluctantly. 'She said witches are just ordinary people like you and me.'

29

ISABELLA

SUN SIGN: LEO ♌

CONFLICTING SUN SIGN: PISCES ♓

Leos love drama and limelight.

They don't like their friends to outshine them . . .

Madre de Dio. Acted out of my socks there! Was fan-bloody-tastic! And Snot gives me a mingy B-minus. I tell you, he'll be *begging* my forgiveness when I'm the new Catherine Zeta Jones. His judgement's as criminal as his checked shirts coz that baldy zero Lizzie Brownarse landed an A-star. For what? Being herself. Something well dodgy there. Makes me think there could be *some* truth in all the daft hocus-pocus Nevin keeps banging on about.

She was at it again before we even left the drama room.

'Doesn't our Lizzie know a thing or two about a thing or two when it comes to witches? Even Snot said she was acting like she wasn't acting. Huh, huh?' Nevin's muttering away while I'm shoving past her. All I want to do is get shot of drama and home but there's a bloody bottleneck at the class door, isn't there? All the gormless blokes in 4C crowding not just Lousy Lizzie, but the frigging *Gerbils*, bigging them up.

'This shouldn't be happening. You acted far better, Bella. We all did,' Nevin's hissing down my lug while me, Jan and Mags are busy bulldozing through the Gerbil Appreciation Society. All right. She has a point, but I'm in no mood for a post-mortem. *Take your one-track conversation and rejoin the rejects,* I feel like screaming because Nevin's chasing me across the school yard now. Waving her drama jotter. Shouting out her own lousy drama grade to try and cheer me up.

'C-minus, Bella. Same as Jan and Mags. That makes you gang swot,' she whoops, thinking she's sassy. But she's not. She's just SO in my face, it's *killing* me. I know I should bite my tongue, but I've just about had it with her.

'What *gang* would that be, Nevin? We don't have a gang, and if we do, who's saying you're in it?' I kick off, and believe me, there's plenty more where that came from. I'd have covered rejects and losers and spud-u-likes for sure. Glad I didn't.

Coz suddenly the only reason I've tholed Nicky Nevin at all is on the scene. When I hear Luke's luscious voice it even seems worth it. Though I can't *believe* what he's asking.

'Seen Lizzie, Nick?' he wants to know. And he *so completely* ignores me. Even though I'm pushing up my boobs as high as they'll go. Even though I'm holding his sad-sack sister's hand. Playing with her friendship bracelet.

'She's meant to be coming home with me. Doing Mum a head massage tonight.' Luke's frowning. Scanning the schoolyard. Looking everywhere but where he should be looking. At me, me, *me* . . .

Nevin's frowning too. Frowning like she's a bad pain somewhere.

'Mum never told *me* Lizzie was coming round,' she says, and her voice is slow and sour and faraway. She stares at her feet. For ages. But when she looks up she's wearing this smirk and her eyes . . . well, they're right *cold.* And bad. Like the eyes of someone dead ordinary in a horror flick who's been possessed

'Anyway, I saw Lizzie going up the back lane with Peter Gibson,' Nevin says. As Luke's sprinting off, she winks at me. But not in a cute way.

'That's her sorted, Bella,' she says, like she deserves an A-star herself now. I put her straight with a wee twist of that friendship bracelet I should never have given her.

'What you doing, Nevin, letting Luka leave me for Lousy?'

I'll give Nevin this. If Snot had seen the look on her face and heard the way she spoke when she answered me, he'd have bumped her up a drama set. But she wasn't acting when she said, 'I'm sorting Lizzie out for you, Bella. Yeah. Gonna prove what she really is. Fancy some of that?'

30
COMPETITION

Now I'd the go-ahead from Isabella to sort Lizzie, I could be on her case big time. So I spent hours in the library, beefing up on everything and anything I could find on the subject of witch-spotting and how to deal with it. Occasionally I came across facts I'd rather not have known. For example, that Margaret, Janet and Isobel were common names for Scottish witches. And a *nicnevin* was a *nick*name for one of Satan's floozies. Now there's a coincidence.

Although, knowledge like this was *not* helpful. Especially when I started feeling *sorry* for all the accused witches in history; poor victimised social scapegoats most of them seemed to be. In the wrong place at the right time.

What *I* needed were snappy facts and practical advice on how to expose a might-be witch like Lizzie Brownie, and, just in case my instincts about her weren't paranoia,

I needed to protect myself from any powers she might really possess.

And I needed this fast.

Because every hour I spent in the library was an hour in which Isabella was losing interest in me. Out of sight, out of mind.

Of course, dimwit here should have sussed that after weeks of texting Luke for nothing and sending me to the Sixth Year Common Room door to ask for him then substituting herself in my place, an alpha gal like Isabella would eventually stop crawling and move on. Which is exactly what happened the week before Hallowe'en.

'Oh, by the way, Nevin, see your big brother? Tell him this,' Isabella called across the schoolyard. Then she seized an imaginary mike from mid-air and bellowed into it, *'I've washed that schoolboy outa my hair and I'm sendin' him on his way.'*

This was the first time she'd spoken to me – or should I say sung at me – in days. She'd taken to disappearing at lunchtimes with Margaret and Janet. Never inviting me along.

'Hey, where've you been, Bella? I've been phoning

and phoning. Got loads to tell you 'bout Luke 'n' Lizzie . . .' I gabbled, following Isabella into school while I'd the chance.

Without breaking stride, Isabella cut me off mid-sentence.

'Talk to the hand, Nevin,' she snapped. 'Before you start, I'm *so* over Luke and way too knackered for another story about him and Lousy. I've been waitressing, right?' She scowled, turning her back, shutting me out.

And here was me, all desperate to tantalise Isabella with the evidence we could use to punish Lizzie Brownie. *Look what I've found out for you, Bella. Listen. You know that lots of witches had birthmarks shaped like animals, just like the one on Lousy's back?*

And healing powers.

And they muttered curses to make bad things happen to people who didn't like them.

Just like Lizzie . . .

Well, what the hell use was all my research now? Isabella had a new preoccupation, as I learned when I hovered round her and Janet and Margaret at break, as unwelcome as a dirty bluebottle trying to settle.

'So the third time Sylvano comes in, he asks Papa if I

can always be his waitress. *Isabellissima* he calls me.'

'And he doesn't mind you're a schoolie?'

'You're mince-for-brains, Mags. D'you think he knows that? I'm eighteen when you meet him, OK?'

'Show us his picture again, Bella. Phewwarrrr!'

I glimpsed the photo Mags and Janet were slavering over. Blond footballer with a six-pack in a pair of brief briefs. Bulges in all the right places.

Luke's competition.

No.

My competition, I realised as the trio moved off, leaving me alone. Only person I could see without company.

The Gerbils, violins in one hand, sheet music in the other, passed me as if I was a ghost.

And Peter Gibson, *my* Peter Gibson, was wooing Molly Mone now. Buying her a cupasoup.

Even Luke didn't stop to talk to me. He didn't even notice me in his haste to join the girl waiting for him at the noticeboard.

'*There* you are, Lizzie.'

Yeah. There she was. Encircled by all Luke's Six Year mates now. And you know what was really galling? As Lizzie stood next to my brother, and rose on her tiptoes to mutter something private that made him sling his arm round her, I could see they looked *right* together.

So I'd no option. I had to do what I had to do.

31
MALEFICE

No. As I figured it I'd no option, especially as Isabella and Margaret and Janet completely ignored me the rest of that day. Even in drama, when I was in their discussion group they ignored me. And Isabella did to me what I'd done to Lizzie Brownie in music a few weeks back. She took her chair and edged it away. Deliberately. Obviously. Then launched into this discussion about what she wanted the others to wear on their treble date with Sylvano and his first-division mates.

I felt *so* not there. Could've stripped to my thong and lapdanced for Snot and who'd've noticed?

There I sat, in my bubble of silence, listening to other people connecting, and I thought to myself, I have to do something about this.

So, instead of going home, I headed into the busy West End of the city.

Daylight was already fading into the gloom of a drizzly

autumn night. On the main street, every shop radiated a pumpkin-coloured glow from its Hallowe'en display, spray-paint ghosts and crepe paper witches leering from lantern-lit windows. For the first time in donkey's – last time I'd done this would have been with *old* Mum: her power shopping, me begging her to slow down – I actually studied every one, my eyes roving the parade of black cats and broomsticks.

The last shop on the main street was a greengrocer's. Being a wee independent, the razzmatazz in its window wasn't quite so dazzling as some of the bigger shops, just the inevitable butchered pumpkins grimacing in a circle around a mountain of monkey nuts. Poking through the pile were skeleton bones – plastic, of course, though in the gloom they glowed realistic enough to make me look closer just to double-check. That's when a movement caught my eye. Above the slag-heap of nuts, hung from invisible wire, a grotesque rubber face, cruel and warty, girned at me through a curtain of wispy grey hair. The mask had eyes that flashed on and off, piercing me in a red laser one moment, empty holes the next.

I stood hypnotised, held in the battery-operated gaze of the crone above me, not even blinking when a couple of kids jostled me aside.

'Hey, now *there's* a decent witch,' the boy guffawed to the girl.

'She's looking at me,' she squealed in reply.

'Come on, you two. Home.' A woman, trackled with shopping, glanced at the window display. She shuddered.

'Doesn't everything feel macabre tonight? Must be the rain,' she said to me, herding her children away.

Macabre. I shuddered myself, the after-image of the witch's eyes splintering into slivers that danced in front of me as I turned up an old cobbled lane. There were no streetlights here and in the gloaming it seemed darker than night, the looming walls of tenement back greens closing in. It was raining harder too, at least harder than I'd noticed on the main street. My feet slithered and skited on the wet of the uneven stones beneath me.

Why am I doing this? I thought, peering ahead through the downpour. Apart from a cat, which leapt from its wall almost as quickly as my heart did to my mouth when its silent shadow slinked my path, I couldn't see another soul.

Behind me the rush of homebound traffic whooshing in the wet, and the bustle of Friday shoppers faded the closer I drew to the mews cottage at the end of the lane.

The only sound louder than the rain was my own uneven breathing.

You don't need to do this. Forget it! a Luke-like voice warned. Stupid shop wasn't even open, the door refusing to yield when I pushed. What was I thinking of anyway? Sloping down here to find real hardcore magic and punish Lizzie Brownie. Was I crazy? Best thing I could do right now was head home and get used to the way things were going to be for me now that Isabella was scunnered with me. Prepare to move on with my life . . .

I *had* actually moved on, turning from the mews, when a spotlight clicked on above me. Must have caught a sensor, I realised, squinting at the Gothic black scroll of the sign I hadn't seen in the dark.

Malefice

it read in huge letters, the smaller sign creaking from the first offering a clue to the nature of the shop's wares.

Everything occult.

I heard the bell chiming inside the shop: an un-occult electronic *bing bong* when the spotlight activated, warning its owner that there was someone outside. Even as I hurried away, back down the lane, I knew a second light had flicked on, and a key was turning. I was still walking away at this point. Believe me.

And I nearly escaped; nearly managed to make everything, this whole story, end differently.

End here.

Except.

I turned when this cheery voice called, 'Hey. Don't go. You must be desperate to trail up here in this weather.'

And the girl grinning at me through the rain was so friendly – 'Hey, you're soaked. Give us your jacket. Look like you'd fancy a hot chocolate?' – that I followed her inside.

And although the occult bookshop was called Malefice, there was nothing in the least *macabre* about it (unless the Ikea look creeps you out). Spookiest thing was hearing Malefice's proprietor introduce herself as 'Elvira', which I had to admit *was* a witchy name. Didn't suit her though. Elvira seemed too scatty for a name like that.

She'd one of those little girl voices that tinkled like the jingle-jangle bangles she wore. Long hair like Meg White, except dyed purple. It matched her velvet flares. I was chuffed to bits at the warm smile she gave me when she asked my name. As if – and how often had this happened to me? – she genuinely, *genuinely* liked me from the off.

'Nicky? Suits you,' and then she asked solemnly, 'So what brings you here, Nicky?'

And I told her.

What the hell have I done? I was panicking half an hour later as I ran down Elvira's lane and shoved my way through crowds of happy-hour revellers to catch my bus home.

Elvira had promised me that everything would succeed, but to tell the truth her tone by then had made my stomach swoop from my boots to my throat and I thought she was pushing her kookiness over the edge of flaky into something darker altogether when she laid her hand on my head and chanted *Thy will be done*. Not *exactly* in her jingle-jangle voice either!

But there must have been *something* in all that good luck Elvira wished me because Mum let me off lightly –

way too lightly, I realise now – for being four hours late. All she said was, 'Where on *earth* have you been, Nicola? Dad's away to the library to find you. Luke's been back to the school . . .'

'Dad's home?'

I suppose that could have explained why Mum didn't mow me down. She was actually smiling.

'Isn't it great? Dad swapped his shift with someone who wants home for Hallowe'en. So where were you?'

I didn't even need to lie.

'Research,' I told Mum. 'Hallowe'en project.'

'Oh, you're a good girl,' Mum kissed me in relief just as Luke burst in and charged me, face like thunder.

'Where the hell have you . . .?'

'It's all right, Luke,' Mum interrupted him. Wheeling herself between us to referee, she took my hand for the first time in ages. She raised it proudly, like I'd finally won something.

'Nicola was studying,' she beamed. 'Imagine us thinking she was up to no good!'

32

BAD MAGIC

'Easy peasy, lemon squeezy. '

Elvira had squealed and clapped her hands in glee when I described the one thing Isabella hated most about herself. Sounded like a wee kid. A freak-you-out wee kid though, because the longer I stayed in her company, the older I realised she was. Her neck crêpey, her hands wrinkled. The long purply hair growing in white at her parting.

'I'll just consult my grimoire,' that wee kid's voice piped while she unlocked – yeah, *unlocked* – this leatherbound book of spells which sat on a lectern.

'All you have to do now, Nicky,' Elvira assured me, 'is heal Isabella's skin and she'll be in your debt.'

Easy peasy, lemon squeezy, I chanted to myself as I phoned Isabella the next morning. My handsweat was on the receiver.

It's rung out four times.

She'll see my number and won't pick up.

Give up on all this, Nicky. You're pathetic, I cringed inside, lowering the phone.

Until . . .

'Hey, Nicky.'

I couldn't believe it. Isabella wasn't exactly trilling the Hallelujah Chorus but she didn't sound peeved either. Rather, she seemed flat. Definitely not her usual who's-the-daddy self.

'Y'OK Bella?'

'Yeah . . . S'pose.'

'How'd it go last night? With Sylvano.'

Here was a new aural experience for me: Isabella actually *sighing.* In dejection.

'It's my bloody skin, Nick. Really flared up last night. Couldn't go out with Sylvano looking like the Elephant Man. Dunno what the hell I'm gonna do.'

Hearing all this from *bella* Isabella, I'd a temporary problem with my own face. It seemed to be splitting itself open like a dropped pumpkin.

'This is freaky,' I told her, amazed at how different my voice sounded when I'd the upper hand, 'but that's *exactly* why I'm phoning you . . .'

* * *

I tell you, Isabella wasn't exaggerating about her affliction: beneath her fedora and Jackie O sunnies, her entire brow area jutted out *à la* Frankenstein's monster.

'Please don't stare, Nicky,' Isabella begged – unnecessarily, quite frankly – when Mama ushered me into her bedroom. Curtains were shut and scarves were draped over her lamps, giving the whole scene a scarred-beauty-who-can't-face-the-world vibe.

'Not looking. Just here to sort this,' I told her. And I'm not kidding, you wanna have heard the way nondescript Nicky Nevin was suddenly talking the talk! I knew fine, as I handed over the spell Elvira had copied from her grimoire last night, that Isabella was keeking over her sunnies at me with new – well, not exactly *respect,* but interest. It was a start.

'What this? Spell To Heal Bad Skin,' Isabella read.

'Listen,' I explained quickly. 'I can stop the bad stuff that's happened to us. I've talked to someone who gave me this skin spell. Swore it works. And she told me how to make that *witch* quit working bad magic on us. We'll need Janet and Mags though . . .'

Isabella didn't heed a blind word of my spiel. All she

cottoned on to was *skin spell,* before she cut me short, finger-clicking to gee me into action:

'Right. I need two apples, Nicky. Go ask Mama. Papa'll run us to Merlock coz we're meant to bury one of the apples where enchanted water lies. That drowny pool Groat dragged us to'll do, yeah? Bloody hell! That's a coincidence, yeah? It's where all this crap started, innit?'

Hey. Can you *believe* things were going my way at last? Like 'magic' you could say.

One minute I was raiding Isabella's fruit bowl, the next I was squatting in squelch beside the Drowning Pond.

Isabella – completely Looby-Loo she looked. Not that I told her! – was rubbing circles into her forehead with an apple big Margaret had split with one twist of her mighty wrists. Janet and I held the corner of the page Elvira had copied from her grimoire. We were all chanting this spell written there:

Goddess of Nature, accept this sacred fruit of your earth as my gift.
May your gift to me be my beauty restored.

We chanted three times. Felt weird. Four of us working

magic like we meant it. Well, two of us really, because to be honest, Janet and Margaret gave about as much attention to this ritual as they'd given Snot when they *Hubble bubble toilet troubled* for him. I caught Mags rolling her eyes, Janet suppressing a yawn. Isabella and I made up for them though, both of us displaying (and I tried not to think about this one) the same taking-care-of-business earnestness as Lizzie and Caroline and Yvonne when they'd played *their* witchy scene from the good old Scottish play.

Course they'd only been *acting*.

Here *we* were, on Gallow Hill. Casting a spell. For real. Invoking a pagan spirit.

The thought of that zigzagged a shiver through me like I was up to . . . well, something *wrong*.

'Feel any different, Bella?' Margaret asked sceptically when Isabella stopped rubbing her face.

'*Think* you might be less lumpy already,' Janet added, failing to look or sound convinced.

'Elvira swore it would work,' I chipped in quickly. Here was the first blip in a situation that had kept the mood civil so far. But now it was clear from the arched symmetry of four raised eyebrows that Margaret and

Janet were thinking, Why has Nevin dragged us all up here exactly? This is bollocks.

I forced myself to smile into their glares.

'Now we've to bury the apple Isabella's rubbed on her skin, and water it –'

'Using what, Nevin?'

'D'you bring your trowel . . .'

'. . . or a watering can?'

'And there's no way I'm diggin' anything,' Isabella was scowling now, disliking the tacky sensation of drying apple juice on her skin.

'We'll break the nails, Bella,' Janet and Margaret pursed, fluttering their fingers.

The atmosphere on top of Gallow Hill was changing, time running out for me faster than a Pop Idol's fifteen minutes. Quickly I dug into my trouser pocket for the charms Elvira suggested I should buy before I left Malefice.

'What's this, Nevin?' asked Isabella gracelessly, picking one of the three objects from my palm. 'Plastic junk sprayed silver. Find it in a lucky bag?'

'Why you givin' us two wee hearts joined together, Nevin?' sneered Margaret, blowing Janet an air kiss. 'Trying to tell us something?'

'It's a talisman,' I began to explain. 'Called a Luckenbooth brooch . . .'

'Hate brooches,' interrupted Janet.

'Me too, Mags. They're for grannies.'

I tried again. 'They'll protect you from evil. You pin it near your left thigh.'

'What the hell for?'

Janet's snort smarted more painfully than the gift she flung back at my face. I'd to drop my head to hide tears.

'You're gonna need it when we're sorting Lousy out. You should put it on while I finish off here.'

With one hand I offered the Luckenbooth brooch again. My other hand, meanwhile, dug the mushy earth, scooping until there was a hole deep enough to bury the apple halves Isabella had used. Above me I sensed an exchange of glances between the others as I went about finishing what I'd started.

It was tricky collecting the pond-water I needed in one cupped hand to complete Elvira's spell. Maybe that was why Isabella took the rejected brooch from me and gave it back to Janet.

'Put it on, Jan,' she commanded. Then she crouched down beside me.

'My skin's stopped louping since I rubbed that apple on it, Nicky,' she mumbled, barely audible beneath the splash of her hands dipping the water. 'Tell us what else you want to do up here,' she added, nodding me to my feet.

It was now or never. As I cleared my throat, my scalp prickled from the menace in what I was about to suggest.

'There's a witch using magic on us. We need to stop her,' I said, and there must have been *something* about my tone of voice because Janet and Margaret looked from me to each other then pinned their Luckenbooth brooches to their jeans in a fumble.

Here was the chance to shine and, boy, for once in my life did I do my best to put on a show! I spun questions faster than a juggler twirls plates on poles:

Who have we seen and heard muttering before horrible things happen to us?

Who's managed to hook the one guy you want, Isabella?

Who knows all about healing potions?

Who admitted her gran's gran's gran's gran was some kind of witch?

Who wrote the creepiest essay you've ever heard?

My questions. Man, they were so *easy peasy, lemon*

squeezy, weren't they? One solitary glaringly obvious answer to them all. Why then did Margaret and Janet persist in frowning glaiketly from me to each other as if I was speaking in tongues?

I practically had to spell it out.

'Who's had it in for us since we noticed her nits? Baldy? Scadgy? Always muttering?'

'Oh, you mean Lizzie?' Realisation dawned slowly on Margaret, but I didn't wait for Janet to catch up.

'That the one! She *definitely* hexed us when we came pond dipping here.'

'D'you think Nicky's right? Naw!' Margaret gawped, swinging round to gauge Isabella's reaction to my suggestions.

'The giveaway's your skin, Isabella.' I urged. 'Witches were *always* giving people boils. *And,* Janet, they'd steal something you wore and cast a spell on it to make you ill or lame.'

'Hey. Like what happened to Mags.'

'Hear that, Bella? She's saying Lousy made me barf my guts.'

'Exactly,' I said, literally applauding Janet's and Margaret's support. Time for my grand finale.

'All that *mutter mutter mutter* was Lizzie working malefice . . .'

'Doing what, Nevin?' Isabella scowled as she turned towards the Drowning Pond, twisty-mouthing the word she didn't understand: *malefice.*

I explained quickly, 'It means witchcraft. From Latin. That's what Lizzie'd've been accused of during the Great Scottish Witchhunt . . .'

I had to pause. I'd been laying my case against Lizzie so urgently that my temples throbbed. Isabella seized on my desperation.

'Cool the beans, Nevin,' she sneered, panting into my face. 'You're creeping us out, talking Latin and casting spells. Let's split. I'm cold.'

Throwing the words carelessly over her shoulder Isabella turned away. She cleeked arms with Margaret and Janet.

'Come if you're coming, Nevin. Papa can drop you home . . .'

Drop you home . . .

Drop you . . .

I tell you, I wasn't ready to be dropped anywhere.

'Hey, Isabella!'

She was halfway across the wooden bridge of the Drowning Pond. As I stood at the water's edge and called her name, my reflection on its barely moving surface mimicked me just as Isabella had done moments before. Arms outstretched, I was begging.

'D'you not care that Lizzie charmed Luke from you?' A languid ripple on the pond carried my challenge to her. 'We should punish her. In this pool. Get him back.'

33

MARGARET

SUN SIGN: ARIES ♈

Aries are attracted to dangerous situations.

They can be harsh and nasty . . .

'What the hell's Bella doing now? Thought we were leaving?'

Jan was so stoked when Bella turned back for *more* of Nevin's pathetic mumbo jumbo that her cry sent all these big black horror-flick birds flapping out the trees round the pond. Sounded like they were cawing at Bella.

What are you playing at, you spam? This is ludicrous! Let's go shopping.

I mean, OK, I could understand how Nevin persuaded Bella we all had to come up here today. If my coupon was as bad as Bella's I'd be tempted to rub my granny's skitters, let alone apples over my face if I thought it'd cure my zits. Where's the harm? Giving some olde worde charm a shot is one thing.

But other stuff Nevin seemed to have all planned out . . .

I thought – to myself at first, by the way, coz Bella would freeze me out permo if she knew I'd soft notions like this – that the things Nevin lined up for Lizzie were not just barking, but cruel. And sick.

Didn't a No Go Area like Lizzie have enough problems without a posse like us on her case? We should have let her be.

But of course, in the end we went along with everything because me and Jan always do. Even though, between you, me and Janet, Bella was losing the plot. Letting that numpty Nevin brainwash her.

'So what d'you want us to do next?' Bella was actually *consulting* Nevin by the time Jan and I were beside the Drowning Pond again.

And to have heard Nevin you'd have sworn she was some kind of expert.

'First we break Lizzie's powers so she can't cast spells any more,' says Nevin, moving things along faster than the time it took me to score in last year's netball finals. 'And *then,'* Nevin went on, and when she spoke her voice was . . .

Well.

Weird, Jan said. Afterwards.

Bad, I said.

'And disturbing. Like you're dealing with someone who's not the full shilling.'

Jan and I both agreed on that.

And that Nevin was *desperate*. Ready to sell her frigging *soul* to keep in with Bella.

Yeah, we both thought that.

34
AND THEN . . .

The Drowning Pond was watchful as a black, unblinking pupil when I leaned over the bridge to peer into its depths before I answered Isabella. Nothing seemed to be moving on its surface. No darting skaters, no zigzagging water-mites. One of those still autumn days of low-watt daylight. Even the lily pads, floating like upturned faces, gazed frozen from the water. And no birds cried. And no leaves rustled on any of the tall trees leaning in towards me on Gallow Hill.

I remember that.

You'd think nature itself was holding its breath. Eavesdropping.

'And then, Nevin?' Bella geed me, so I took one big, deep breath and plunged.

'We swim Lizzie in here,' I said.

Evil.

Wrong.

A great shiver ran through me. You know that sensation that sears you when you bite down on silver foil? It was worse than that, I tell you, enough to make me rear back from the wooden bridge I gripped as though it was suddenly electrified. And I shrivelled inside.

Nicky! Luke's voice gasped somewhere in my head as though he'd tapped the same power source as I had. *How can you behave like this*?

But nothing else happened. The world kept turning. No one told me to stop.

35

JANET

SUN SIGN: CANCER ♋

Lucky gemstone: Pearl or moonstone, which

will protect from poison.

Cancerians are prone to stomach and

digestive tract problems.

They often suffer from eating disorders . . .

Mags 'n' me are beginning to wonder if Bella's plukes are pressing into the bits of her brain that help her think straight. Because Nevin's gone from rubbing plukes away with apples to planning a *drowning* on Hallowe'en. And Bella's totally buying it! Not to mention Nevin's extra-large hot chocolate with marshmallows and whipped cream in Merlock's visitor centre.

'This just isn't right,' Mags whispers to me while we're stumping up for our own drinks. And she's spot on. I mean Bella's giving Nicky so much attention she doesn't even bother when Alan – remember that cute forest ranger? – brings his coffee to the next table.

'Hey, booty at three o'clock,' I alert Bella.

'Givin' you the eye. Ranger danger,' Mags adds with one of her special whispers. It's louder than the frother on the cappuccino machine.

'Grow up, eejits,' Isabella snarls. Not for one second does her attention waver from Nevin.

'. . . So before we swim Lizzie in the pond we scratch her across the brow,' Nevin's explaining and – omigod, I can't believe this is happening, but *right* in front of Alan Bella's lifting up her fringe and *acting out* what Nevin's telling her. She's slashing her index finger across all her zits, putting the poor guy right off his Garibaldi!

'So the scratch we give Lizzie *has* to bleed?' Bella asks, and I get a wee instinct that cute ranger's listening in. His head's tilting towards us, and when I glance over he's stirring and stirring at his coffee. Like you'd do when you're trying not be there.

Nevin must have twigged the ranger's flapping luggies too because she covers her mouth with her hand and mumbles.

'Yeah, Bella. We make Lizzie bleed so any powers she

has are broken. She can't curse us –'

'Whit?' Mags expodes. She's leaning across the table towards Nevin. Cupping a hand to her ear. 'Her *shower's* broken?' she booms.

'Not *shower*; her *powers*. Retard!' Isabella sneers, cuffing Mags on the side of her head. 'We bleed the magic out Lizzie, that right, Nicky?' Isabella double-checks.

'Sor-*ry*,' Mags huffs. 'Nicky's mumbling away like a wee witch herself.'

'Aye, speak up,' I agree. Though frankly, I've had enough, and I can't keep schtoom any longer.

'How're we meant to scratch Lizzie anyway? Or get her up to *this* park without being caught? *Hey Lizzie, fancy comin' to Merlock so we can drown you?* Welcome back to the real world, Bella, coz that ranger's looking right over at you. We gunna speak to –' I'm clicking my tongue at the next table.

'He's quality, Bella. And if you don't want him . . .' Mags chips in, licking her chops like a hungry vixen.

'. . . then we'll have him. And he's way fitter than Nicky's schoolie brother. Fancy your chances, Bella? Bella? BELLA!'

I'm digging hard at Bella's ribs now coz cute Alan's not

even pretending to pretend he's not interested. His eyes are all over me and Mags, lingering as per usual over Bella – not, I would say in a sexy way, but I reckon being a man of the world he's just playing things cool.

'Hey, we're in, Mags,' I hiss out the corner of my mouth.

'Work it, Bella. We've pulled. He's coming over,' Mags is squealing, so excited she squeezes Bella's hand.

'Leave it, you hacket boot,' Bella snarls, flinging Mags' hand away so roughly it bounces off the table with a crump. Alan's alongside Bella at this point. And he's leaning down to speak to her. So that must be why his chin lands the backswing of her arm. *Boomph*!

'What the . . .?'

Isabella's punch can't have been *that* hard, but Alan's hands fly to his cute goatee. Shame he's acting more like a big jessie than a power ranger, I'm thinking. Till I notice all this blood running between his fingers.

'Jeez . . .'

When Alan moves his hands, even Bella winces. Something sharp's gashed the gap between his bottom lip and chin.

'What the heck?' Alan grabs a napkin to staunch the blood pouring down his neck. 'Must have talons there . . .'

'Prego!' Now Bella's smiling at Alan, looking more chuffed than sorry for what she's just done to him if you ask me. 'I'd this in my hand,' she tells him, flashing her Luckenbooth brooch. 'Pin must be sharp.' She's shrugging, eyes glittering. *'Really sharp*. Sorry again.' Now she's purring. Turning to wink at Nevin.

'We'll scratch Lizzie with this,' she beams, though her face fair turns to thunder when Alan taps her on the shoulder.

'Knew I'd seen you before. You're that girl whose skin flared up,' he reminds her. 'My wife's a medic. Told her about you . . .'

Oh dear. Was *that* the wrong chat-up line?

Bella was raging.

'See that Lizzie witch; she's getting dunked bigtime. *My wife's a medic. Told her about you*. Am I a bloody specimen in a jar?' she storms. Told us to forget our hot chocs. We were all going back up Gallow Hill for a proper recce of the Drowning Pond.

Me 'n' Mags were not pleased. We were in mourning about Alan being out of bounds.

'What a tease, Bella. *Wife*. D'you hear him say "wife"?'

Mags laments.

'Way too hot to be caught –' I begin when Bella grabs the pair of us by the collar. Hauls us down the bank of the pond till water's lapping our tootsies.

'Look at my face. Concentrate. We're not here to catch men,' Isabella warns. 'We're making a witch pay. *Capisce*?'

'All right, I'm with you,' bleats Mags. There was water in her stookie now.

'Jan?'

'In,' I say. Sullen as I dare with Bella's nails digging my neck. But then I think, Stuff this, and I blurt, 'But Nevin hasn't told us how we're getting Lousy up here. Whole thing's bloody *stupid*. Why you into this mumbo-jumbo? It's sick, innit, Mags?'

'Totally.' Mags does her nodding dog impersonation and keeps it going for so long that she probably hypnotises Bella, because she finally grins at us. She's shaking her head like she's clearing it of unwanted thoughts.

'You're right enough, Mags,' she chuckles, thumbing a number into her moby. '*Swimming a witch,* for God's sake, Nevin! What planet you on? Papa'll drop you somewhere, coz we're going into town.'

Now it was Nevin's turn to be miffed. Me and Mags

and Bella are walking away arm in arm. We've left her staring into the gunky Drowny Pond. Punching the fist of her left hand into the palm of her right and, this is God's honest truth, she was actually *chanting* to herself:

Self-belief doth magic make make, self-belief doth magic make, self-belief doth magic make . . .

'She's freaking me out, Bella,' I'm shivering.

'Let's *go*!' Mags says, the pair of us tugging Bella downhill more quickly now.

Then comes this *sound* that stops us dead. From Nevin. A sort of screech that rises up behind us, sending all the poor wee birdies in the trees flapping into the sky.

'Why you so scared, Bella?'

Man, this was *not* funny any more.

'Just come with us,' I'm plucking at Bella's arm.

'Stay,' Nevin's voice seems to echo round the whole of Merlock Park. 'You'll get Luke back,' it whispers, and when I turn, Nevin's there. Right there. Like one of those characters who never dies in a horror film you'd never watch alone. Nevin was staring into Bella's eyes. Holding her hand out.

And Bella took it.

36

FALSE FRIENDS

Two days later we were filing into music. I could have had my pick of any seat near Mrs Jackson's desk, but I joined the lone figure already up the back.

'Hi, Lizzie,' I smiled warmly, though inside I was feeling uglier than the ugliest pumpkin glowing on the Main Street.

'Hi.'

'Hi.'

'Hi.'

Three more ugly pumpkins girned at Lizzie. All part of The Plan. We'd allowed ourselves two days to creep into Lizzie's trust with measured dods of civility, careful she didn't become *too* suspicious. Then it would be GOTCHA.

'Splish splash!'

'Witch overboard,' as Janet and Margaret put it. With no more than a bit of virtual nipple-twisting from Isabella they'd come round to the idea that it'd be a gas punishing

Lizzie for the sake of their leader's love life.

'Mind if we sit here? Not keeping that chair for a pal?' I asked Lizzie, so airily insincere Janet nearly blew it. Her snort was louder than a sinusitis-stricken sow with a megaphone in her trotter.

'Cut it out, Pikey. Low key. Remember?'

Two chairs away, I caught Isabella's whispered warning to Janet. I noticed her press two fingers hard over the bump on Janet's skirt where her Luckenbooth brooch was pinned to her knickers. On my instruction we were all wearing them for protection.

'Know what we're doing in music today, Lizzie?' I masked Janet's yelp of agony by trilling. Carelessly conversational. Could have been asking anyone.

There was a beat of hesitation before Lizzie shrugged. 'Dunno. Singing, I hope . . .'

She was suspicious, natch, but I'd allowed for that, almost relaxing as Lizzie's green eyes searched my face, and seconds later I was giving myself a virtual pat on the back. Lizzie was pointing to the board.

'Look. Handel, "Where e'er you walk". We *are* singing, Nicky.'

Having broken the ice successfully with Lizzie at the start of the period, I deliberately didn't give her any more chat, concentrating on putting my heart and soul into the song we were learning. I didn't even ask her if she'd heard from Luke, who was away all week on some rugby tour. When the lunch bell rang I tossed her a non-committal, 'See ya,' then chummed Isabella to the bogs so she could check her plukes before they went on public display in the ref.

I was in a good mood, humming to myself till I saw Mags and Janet collapsed against the bog sinks. They were clutching their bellies. Pointing at me.

'This is you 'n' Lizzie, Nevin,' Janet panted, jutting out her chin and casting her eyes heavenwards, a simpery martyred face on her.

'Where e'er you squawk . . .' she trilled, hideously off-key.

'People beg you please stop,' Margaret joined in. She conducted herself in a tuneless bass warble.

'Nicky 'n' Lizzie. Cats' chorus. In't they, Bella?' Margaret's chortle swelled then died as Isabella ignored her mimicry. Wasn't like her. Normally, as lunchtime began, Bella'd be like a big cat herself. Any other female approaching the mirrors was fair game, assessed then devoured by a few acid whispers while Isabella regrouted her own forehead.

'Wasting your time with a nose like that, hen.'

'Make-up won't hide those chins, lardy girl.'

Today, however, Isabella was focused on her own reflection, eyes two dark pools beneath the shadow of her heavy fringe. There was a stillness about her like you get in those music videos where the central figure doesn't move although everything rushes by in fast-frame. Her self-absorption disconnected her from the ever-changing line-up bobbing in, out, round about her to check their hair, their lippy or wash their hands. Something was going on with Isabella because ten minutes after the bogs had cleared she was still eyeballing herself, barely blinking. Hadn't said a word.

'Going for eats now, Bella?' Margaret's belly growled her question. Tapping her watch face she cocked her head for Janet to follow her to the door.

'Are we alone? Check.' Isabella spoke at last. 'CHECK.' Isabella's command ricocheted from the tiled walls when Margaret didn't plunge to her knees fast enough to peer under each cubicle door.

'Clear, Bella.'

'Right. Look at my face.'

Isabella jack-knifed over the washbasin in front of her then straightened to her full height, interlaced fingers covering her forehead so we couldn't see it. Slowly she swept her hands over the top of her skull, exposing her face.

She looked completely grotesque, by the way, having stretched her hair back so tight that all the skin round her temples had gone with it, like a facelift too far. Her nostrils flared, and above them her eyes were upturned slits, their pupils two glittery marbles sliding from side to side.

'Och, Bella,' Janet tutted. She'd barely glanced at Isabella's forehead.

'Nae luck,' agreed Margaret, daring to peer a little longer. 'Nevin's spell didn't work then. No point in scratching Lizzie now. Coming for lunch? Macaroni cheese . . .'

Without letting her eyes drop Isabella kicked at Margaret's bad ankle.

'Forget your belly and LOOK,' she yelled, rounding on me now, her hands still dragging her hair back.

'See, Nevin . . . No, *see*, Nevin.' She loomed close enough for our eyebrows to knit.

'Haven't had a new spot since I rubbed my face. And in music my skin went all tingly and tight. Must be your spell, those apples, that brooch –'

'Working,' I said, praying I was too out of focus for her to read my lie.

Completely kidding herself Isabella was, see. OK, her skin might have dried up a bit, but even a science retard like me could figure that apple juice would be an astringent. And Isabella's poor forehead had most likely stopped erupting because Elvira's spell had ended with the instruction: *Your skin leave bare and touch it not, Let Mother Nature heal the spot.*

So Isabella'd given her poor coupon a break from being picked and squeezed whenever she passed a mirror. And laying down her foundation trowel for a few days, she'd let her skin breathe. Simple as that, and any dermatologist would have given Isabella the same advice as Elvira's spell: no make-up, no zit-picking. There was no *proper* witchcraft involved in a healing remedy like that. No magic cure for Isabella's acne either. Plenty of forthcoming action bubbled under the surface of her skin. Up close as I was you could see the pores stretched over the tell-tale bumps of eruptions-in-waiting. But was I going to break the bad news?

Was I wheech.

Not when Isabella was kissing me on both cheeks.

'*Mia cara,* what do we do next?' she asked me, taking my arm to cross to the ref.

Self-belief doth magic make.

37

SCRATCHING THE WITCH

So, fed by an entire lunch-hour of Isabella's undivided attention, I was convinced that doing what I was about to do to Lizzie Brownie was a service to mankind.

'Hi,' I greeted her. Careful to scan the noticeboard and not her face, I checked that the pin-tip of my Luckenbooth brooch jutted beyond my thumb.

'Crisp?' I said, offering Lizzie my bag of cheese 'n' halitosis.

Lizzie's green eyes were on me. *Can I trust you?* I knew they were thinking, so I met them directly as I gave the crisps a tempting rattle. *They're not poisoned.*

Lizzie smiled.

'Ta, Nicky,' she said, the ragged scab on her healing pinkie catching on the edge of the bag.

Totally actually hideous, I shuddered, watching Lizzie lift a crisp to her mouth, then – oh, better than at rehearsal – I made myself freeze.

'Don't move,' I whispered.

Leaned in.

'Wasp,' I mouthed.

I'd my thumb swiped across Lizzie's brow before she even knew what I was warning her about. The Luckenbooth pin must have been sharper than Old Groat's tongue because it slit Lizzie's bare forehead like a warm knife cutting Lurpak.

Easy peasy, lemon squeezy.

'It's gone.' I let my smile widen, then drop. 'Shit. I've scratched you.' Delving into my schoolbag to hide my grin, I kidded on I was looking for a hankie.

'Damn. *Help*!'

As planned, my holler brought a certain trio sauntering to Lizzie's aid.

'What's wrong?' Isabella asked, giving me double thumbs up behind Lizzie's back while Mags and Jan threw giveaway theatrical winks.

'My fault,' I explained to the others, hoping I didn't sound completely stilted. 'Scratched Lizzie by mistake.'

'Retard,' Isabella scolded me. 'Want us to take you to the nurse, then?'

'Only if it's bad,' Lizzie shrugged.

'It's bad,' I heard Janet mutter as we chummed Lizzie to the toilets. 'Bleedin' way more than the ranger guy.'

'Never thought Nevin'd go through with this. It's not right,' said Margaret to Janet from the doorway of the bogs. I'd to turn my tap full blast so Lizzie wouldn't hear them.

'It was an accident. Sorry,' I chanted like my needle was stuck. And to be honest, the more I apologised, the more I meant it. Because my Luckenbooth scratch *had* done way more damage than I intended. A horizontal line oozed across Lizzie's brow.

Should stop this now, I panicked inside. Should tell Isabella we've punished Lizzie enough.

That would have been the right thing to do, wouldn't it?

As I leaned over the sink my lips were mouthing my silent thoughts. I'd to gulp the words away, unable to meet Lizzie's eye when she caught mine over a fresh paper towel.

'Just a scratch, Nicky. Mind you –' She was grinning as she waggled her scarred pinkie at me. 'I'm beginning to think you *do* have it in for me. Better watch myself.'

In the mirror I just caught sight of my guilty-as-sin rabbit-in-the-headlights expression before Isabella elbowed me aside.

'Hope this doesn't scar. You've such good skin,' she said ominously to Lizzie. 'Better let the nurse see it . . .'

This was an order for Janet and Margaret to make themselves useful. As they led Lizzie away, Isabella clamped my face between her hands.

'Can't *believe* you did that. You really are the cool one, Nicky Nevin. So what's next?' she whispered.

And I knew that for the first time I'd *truly* won her respect.

Her admiration.

Her friendship . . .

But who was I kidding?

I wanted to crumple to the floor as Isabella kept smiling into my reflection. Had to grip the sink hard with both hands. Wanted to punch the mirror and smithereen the girl with guilty eyes who was staring into my soul at the other side of the glass.

What have you done? Her accusation screamed inside my head. *Stop now.*

'So what's next?' Isabella repeated. 'The Drowning Pond, yeah?'

Enough's enough. We've gone too far.

That was all I had to say.

Except it took guts.

This was easier:

'Yeah. The Drowning Pond next. I'll ask Lizzie out on Hallowe'en. Say it's to make up for what I've done here. Leave everything to me.'

'Guest of honour you are,' I told Lizzie when she queried the fancy computer invitation I handed her a couple of days later. She frowned deeply as she read, breaking the long scabbed scratch on her forehead until it seeped.

'Sure about this, Nicky?'

'Totally,' I assured her, turning to Isabella and the others as they joined us at the school gates.

'Uhuhuh!' Isabella Beyoncé-ed, *'We're gonna make this a night to remember . . .'* she sang into her ever-handy imaginary mike, circling her index finger at Lizzie as she danced backwards towards Papa's car.

So. It *did* end up here:

Merlock Country Park on Hallowe'en night . . .

38

SWIMMING IN THE DROWNING POND

When our candles blew out at the Drowning Pond the night turned matt black. Clouds veiling any stupid witches' moon. I'm not sure who screeched first into the darkness.

'Bella!'

Could've been Janet, Margaret . . . Lizzie . . . Could even have been me although I reckon my vocal cords petrified along with my legs in those seconds following the kerfuffle of tumbling Lizzie Brownie into the water.

'Bella?'

Hands grappled my arms. Two? Three? Whose? Couldn't tell. All I knew is they tugged me downwards until I slid, unable to stop. Mud yielded to my digging heels, denying me grip, and suddenly icy water was forcing my legs from under me. Floating me. Out from the bank. Out of my depth. I was adrift, my cries turning into gargles as I took in lungfuls of windblown water. It was sour and thick, stringy with pondweed and God knows what else.

'Bella!!!'

That third cry was definitely mine, shrilled as I bobbed free of the last clutching hand on my arm, and felt myself drawn away from the others, a paper boat caught and claimed by a sudden breeze.

'Gonna quit bawling, Nevin, and fish me out,' came Isabella's reply. She sounded more affronted than afraid. 'Can't keep my feet on the ground here. Keep floating up. Ma knickers are wringing and this stupid coat's billowing like a balloon.'

'I'm the same, Bella.'

'My jacket's full of air –'

'It's taking me out –'

'Can't get to the side –'

'Must be a current in here –'

'Pushing my legs off the bottom –'

'Can't stand up –'

'I'm floatin' –'

'Me too –'

I'd Margaret and Janet placed now, bouncing in anxious stereo from opposite sides of the pond. And louder than any twin racket from Mags and Janet, Isabella's shriek soared into the dark sky.

'I'm really wet now. Help me, someone!'

In that moment something terrible dawned on me.

Four bodies were accounted for.

Floating.

Not sinking.

Not drowning.

Safe.

But there'd been no fifth splash. No struggle. No cry for help.

'Lizzie!' I bellowed, no longer fighting the current that buoyed me up but using it, swimming with it to circle the Drowning Pond.

'She's tied up. She'll drown!' I screamed into Margaret's face when my arms wrapped her and not Lizzie.

'Find her!' I shook Janet's bony shoulders, sending her across the pond with a shove.

'Oi, Nevin. Never mind Lizzie. Help *me* out.' Isabella was incredulous. 'You told us Lizzie's a bloody witch. She's meant to float. She'll be fine.'

'She's not a witch. We're the ones floating.'

The sob that carried my admission drained any strength I had left. Suddenly my legs felt clad in frozen armour, not denim, and my trainers set to concrete. More exhausting than anything physical, however, was the weight of my guilt. Ten, fifteen minutes ago Lizzie Brownie, tethered like condemned meat, had looked into my eyes and pleaded for me to put a stop to what we went on and did. I failed her.

'It's all my fault.'

My second admission was a gurgled one and as I made it, I began to sink. Fast. My knackered legs corkscrewing me down and down, deeper than I'd ever have believed the Drowning Pond to be. Don't ask me how long I was under. Felt like a lifetime, all these images passing before my eyes like glimpses of floors in a descending glass elevator. People say that happens, don't they? When you're drowning. The milestones of your life flash by like a slideshow you'll never see again –

First day at school. Sat beside Caroline and Yvonne because they weren't wailing for their mums like I was. Both of them putting their arms round me.

Next slide, please:

A windswept esplanade. My wee legs going round like pistons trying to keep up with Mum on one of our Sunday strolls. *One day you'll be as fit as I am, Nicola. Overtaking me.*

Next slide, please:

Those same wee legs belting me up a station platform. I vault into Dad's arms when I see him coming off the train from Aberdeen after two weeks without him.

Next slide, please:

Luke winking at me from the audience in the school hall. Mum's next to him. Only parent in a wheelchair. In front of the front row. Tears shine in her eyes. She's watching me – I'm the middle of the front row in the choir – singing to her: 'Will Ye No Come Back Again'.

Next slide, please:

Opening my first Valentine knowing it's from Peter Gibson. *You're just right,* it says.

Next slide, please . . .

Who am I kidding?

Nothing from my personal catalogue of vivid memories popped up in the slideshow that played while I was submerged in the Drowning Pond.

I saw things I didn't want to see.

Things that made me shut my eyes and open my mouth in an underwater scream because I could still see them when I tried not to look.

In the murk, many, many bundled shapes floated around me like stones in space. They'd bump each other gently, the force separating them. Graceful as a dance in slo-mo. A trail of rags linked these shapes even when they parted, loose shreds of fabric brushing my face like lingering fingers as each bundle drifted through the water and found a new place to settle on the floor of the Drowning Pond. Every bundle, regardless of its size, was bound the same way, with criss-cross rope tying hands to feet.

And every bundle had a face.

Not a living one though.

Do I have to tell you that the faces were eyeless? Eaten away?

That weeds and slime swam through sockets?

Do I have to tell you what every bundle was?

That none of them were Lizzie Brownie?

Please.

Isn't it enough for me to say that the Drowning Pond

was punishing me before it sent me back to face the consequences of what I'd done?

You see, I wasn't actually drowning. I realised this when my knees struck a sharp edge and my flailing arms passed through the surface of the water and were grabbed. I was being hauled with all the grace of a bloater paid on to the deck of a trawler until my torso was wallowing in muddy shallows. There was a flashlight dazzling my eyes, hands slapping my face.

'Hello. What's your name?'

Before I could lift my head from the gloop I was slurping from, and answer the voice I thought I knew, a weight was slung on top of me. Then another. Any water I'd inhaled was forcefully expelled by the double mass crushing my bones. When something hot and vile was burped up in my ear, I knew Janet and her dodgy stomach had made it out the water. Margaret too, judging by my instant relief when two-thirds of the load on my upper body rolled away in disgust.

And Isabella. I knew she was fine when she booted my backside.

'Some night to remember, Nevin,' she railed, emptying all the water caught in her cuff over me. 'Need my bloody stomach pumped and my phone's knackered.'

The flashlight trained on me was also backlighting Isabella so she seemed to be looming from a great height in swarthy elongated silhouette. Her mac, slick as soaked sealskin, clung to the length and contours of her body and her hair hung waistlong in sleek tendrils, twisted like black barley sugar. She cut an imposing figure. Pallid face. Finger pointed accusingly between my eyes.

'Hey. Let us through here,' one of two men crouching over me interrupted her. His voice carried enough authority to bustle Isabella back a few steps.

'Don't you be disappearing, missy,' he warned her, helping Margaret struggle to her feet. Heaving me upright next. 'We'll we wanting a few answers once we know everyone's safe.'

'Ask *her* then. I'm *off*,' Isabella muttered. Sidling on to the bridge, she tipped the wink to Margaret and Janet that they should follow.

'Hold it. Is everyone out?' The second man, whose voice I thought I'd recognised, swung his zigzagging flashlight momentarily from the surface of the Drowning Pond. It was Alan the ranger, freezing Isabella in guilty torchlight as she tried to escape.

'Hey, I know you. And you,' he cried, sweeping his light round the four of us. His free hand probed his chin. 'I *knew* you were all up to something the other day. What have you done?'

It was me who answered, Alan's torch already searching the surface of the Drowning Pond before I forced the words out. Like he knew what I was going to say.

'There's a girl in there. She's tied up.'

Witches.

Bitches.

I don't know which of the two words Alan spat, because it was swallowed by the insucking gasp as his lower body entered the water.

'Need more lights, Bill,' Alan urged as he waded out. 'Need more people.'

Mags and Janet, give them their due, probably hit the water before I did. No questions asked. I tell you, it was Baltic in there second time around, my already drenched, shocked body chittering enough to whisk up a pondweed mousse. My hands and arms were frozen so numb that I wouldn't have been able to identify a human shape if I'd found one, let alone rescue it.

'Nothing. Still nothing,' Alan gasped, spouting pond

water despairingly. 'How long since she went in? THINK!'

When none of us answered Alan cut through us with a swipe of his hands. Same gesture he'd used to disperse midgies that hot day when we'd first learned about the Drowning Pond . . .

'Get the cops, Bill. This poor girl'll be drowned. LIZZIE!' he shouted, filling his lungs for another dive.

Drowned.

I stared at Alan's upper body dipping the pond in slo-mo one more time.

Lizzie could be *dead.*

D-R-O-W-N-E-D.

And her last moments:

Bound tight. No air. Dark green water filling my lungs. Choking me. No voice now. To cry to my murderers: Help me. Save me. No arms pulling me back into life . . .

My God, could there be a more totally actually hideous way to die?

Just so that *I* could keep in with the in crowd a little longer. Be liked. Belong. Feel interesting. Not plain. Take the lead. Make things *happen.* Change destiny with my powers. Try to make things go my way like they never went my way any more . . .

I couldn't see Mags and Janet clearly any more – they'd splashed beyond range of Bill's flashlight – but I could hear bawling.

'Nicky told us to teach Lizzie a lesson . . .'

'. . . get our own back . . .'

'. . . for what she'd done to us . . .'

'Nicky said Lizzie'd float . . .'

'. . . coz Nicky, *you* told us . . .'

'Yeah, Nicky, *you* told us . . .'

'. . . Lizzie was a witch.'

'Don't you be going anywhere,' Bill warned them. He was trying to keep his torch trained on three different subjects: Alan and me in the water, Jan and Mags at the edge of the Drowning Pond, and the mobile phone in his hand. His poor light seemed to be fading already.

'Can't get a bloody signal the one time I need it,' he tutted, shaking his phone, pointing it in different directions. The torchbeam swung with him:

To the bank.

To the pond.

To the trees.

'Keep trying, Bill. LIZZIE!' Alan dived again, in complete darkness this time.

Because Bill's torch had frozen on the trees.

There was someone there.

39
THE END

'Police are coming,' Bill shouted. 'Whoever's there, stay put.'

Whoever's there . . .

'Bella?' Mags and Janet bleated like lost sheep, but I didn't call out with them. Isabella'd long scarpered. And anyway, even the fleetest glimpse I'd caught of the shape looking down from the same little rise where Lizzie Brownie wandered off that day we went pond dipping was enough for me to know it couldn't be Isabella della Rosa. Not in a million years.

OK. You'll think when I tell you what I'm going to tell you next that I was unravelling . . . Touch of hypothermia plus shock. But I swear . . . what I saw . . . *who* I saw . . .

Look, just hear me out. Then *you* figure it.

For a second, I clocked this figure before everything went dark, but in the moments that followed it was like, well, like *she* – *definitely* a *she* – appeared, not fading but developing like a photograph in a darkroom of night. From negative to substance, reforming into clear focus to become someone I knew.

She had a bare skull. Misshapen, like it had taken some knocks. It topped a slight body bundled in something shiftlike and ill-fitting. This figure slumped like it was old, or done in with life . . .

Isobel Gowdie, I heard myself whisper.

Before me was Lizzie Brownie's incarnation by the Drowning Pond, the Isobel she'd brought to life in her English essay.

She was staring at me. Right at me. Her head was roughly shaved, nicked and bleeding where the razor had slipped. Patches of hair remained here and there, wispy scrub amid purpling bruises and egg-like swellings. There were more bruises on Isobel's cheeks, one long fresh graze slashing the bare skin above her brow. Her lip was split and swollen, tongue probing it through a toothless mouth. Christ, it was *macabre,* though I couldn't look away. Not when the reproachful eyes of Lizzie's Isobel were boring me like a laser, still there on the inside of my eyes when I blinked. And still there when I screamed and turned and tried to thrash my escape through the Drowning Pond.

Isobel! my head-voice freaked out, although that wasn't the name that boomeranged around the trees of Merlock and back to me. *'Lizzie Lizzie LIZZIE!'*

For a few moments I'd the most terrifying thought that I was going to be punished for everything I'd done by having Lizzie's name clang incessantly in my conscience. In Luke's voice. Until I saw Luke himself charging over the rise beside the Drowning Pond, a torch blazing in each hand.

'Lizzie Lizzie Lizzie!' he yelled, and then his cry changed. 'There you are.'

As Luke's light swept over me I thought it was me he'd found, and I cringed. On my belly I crawled towards the nearest undergrowth.

'Thank goodness you're fine,' Luke said. He'd his arms round the figure on the rise. I was so relieved she was alive, I forgot that the last time I'd seen her she was tied and bound and gagged . . .

'Not even wet, Lizzie. Thank God. Isabella's flat out on the path back there. Drenched. She's caught her neck in a rope dangling from a tree. Says it dropped down and tried to choke her. Says you slipped into the water by accident,

Lizzie. And that Nicky's here. Well, if you're listening, Nicky? I saw the invitation you made on the computer. I know what you did . . .'

There are three sides to every story:

Your side.

My side.

And the truth between . . .

40
AFTERMATH

Nearly Christmas and Luke still doesn't speak to me unless he has to.

Won't walk to school with me.

Ignores me in the corridors, even though I'm always on my own.

Our last conversation . . . well, it was him giving me pelters I'll never forget that Hallowe'en night. In front of everyone: Isabella. Margaret. Janet. Lizzie.

How could you do this, Nicky? Just to keep in with your stupid mates . . .

When Luke was done, Bill the older ranger stepped in.

'This is a police matter,' Bill warned the drookit lineup of us before he bundled us into his van. Or it would have been if he'd been able to get through to the law on his mobile or his walkie talkie.

But he couldn't get a line out of Merlock from the

Drowning Pond that Hallowe'en night.

Weird that, don't you think? Not being able to make outside contact.

If I was still making my half-baked claims about Lizzie Brownie being a witch, I'd suggest she was hexing the lines of communication. You see, for some reason, despite what we'd done to her, she was more desperate than any of us that we should leave Merlock Park without a police escort.

'Please,' she begged Bill when he hoiked us into his office and lined us up in front of his desk. 'The girls were just pranking me for Hallowe'en. I'm fine about it.'

While Lizzie spoke, her gaze panned Margaret and Janet and Isabella dismissively, but rested on me. The lightness of her shrug might have been shucking off our night's business as though it weighed less than a bag of magic dust, but Lizzie's stare hit my conscience like a wrecking ball. I gulped in relief when her green eyes turned from me to Alan and Bill.

'Can't you let us go? Please?' Lizzie began. Her voice was low, its tone the same one she used to hypnotise Mum's hands with her oils.

'Don't phone the police. I can look after myself. You can bar us from the park. You'll never see any of us again. We'll never come back.' Lizzie's words tailed off.

Click click click.

A two-bar fire in the centre of the office marked time. Like an automaton Bill's head moved in small jerky intervals with the sound. He was processing Lizzie's request: studying the lineup before him, his lips parting to speak, then clamping shut.

'No. I just can't let this business go,' Bill sighed at last. His eyes had come to rest on Isabella. She was returning his stare, eyelids leaden with defiance. Bill shook his head, lifted his phone.

'Too serious, this carry-on. You with me, Alan?'

Before Alan could cheep, Lizzie was in front of him.

'You'll never see *any* of us again, I said. We will *not* be back,' Lizzie intoned, so close to Alan that he reeled away from her.

'Look. Let's just get them out of here, Bill. Something not right about any of this,' he shuddered, shouldering Luke to one side in his own haste to leave the office.

So at least one good thing came out of a horrible night: I'll never have to deal with Mum – or Dad – knowing what I did. Can't even begin to *imagine* how they'd react.

It's bad enough that they know something happened.

Something cataclysmic enough to make me scuttle for my room whenever Luke's about.

What's the score with you pair? Dad keeps fishing, and for all he's a semi-detached parent, he's come closest to the truth.

'Something went on with green-eyed Lizzie before she left, didn't it? She was a funny lassie. Did anyone ever adopt her? Neither of you know? I thought you were doing a line with her, Luke? And I thought you were a bitty jealous of her, Nicky. She was so good for your mum . . .'

Mum and Dad can probe all they like, but they'll never know what happened at the Drowning Pond on Hallowe'en. Lizzie took care of that before she disappeared.

Once the rangers were done with us that horrible night, Luke drove everyone home. He barely bothered to brake as he offloaded Janet and Margaret.

'Get a move on,' he growled while Isabella footered

with her seat belt, shredding her attempt to thank him for the lift in the shriek of his wheelspin.

Then Luke pulled up outside Lizzie's foster home. Leaned towards her. And she leaned towards him. Made him promise to keep what he knew a secret.

'Swear, Luke,' Lizzie held him by the wrist. 'Say nothing. Ever.' She gave him her green-eyed stare. 'I have to go now.'

'OK. Swear,' Luke promised. Then Lizzie let him peck her goodnight. Shame he didn't snog her properly. If he'd winched her she'd have left her goodbye with someone who really didn't want her out of their life. The parting stroke of her finger on someone who ached for her touch.

Instead of across my forehead.

If Luke had kissed Lizzie then at least one of us would have had a *decent* memory of her.

And it would have robbed her of the breath to say, 'You watch yourself, Nick Nevin.'

But Luke wasn't to know this was the last time he'd ever see Lizzie Brownie.

Wish we could talk about it. Talk about her. Talk about anything . . .

41
CAROLINE

SUN SIGN: SAGITTARIUS ♐

Lucky colours: Blues, purples, white.

Sagittarians see the best in people and don't hold grudges . . .

This is a coincidence. It's like we're psychic or something, but on exactly the same day Yvonne and I both decided we should get Nicky over to sit in Lizzie's old seat in choir.

The way she looked had been bugging us both. So sad. Dead lonely. No one ever talking to her. For weeks she'd spent every break sitting on the same bench in the corner of the yard with her headphones on and her nose in a book. Isabella, who was practically her Siamese twin at the start of term, swanned past with Margaret and Janet to chat up the builders working on the school annexe. We could tell they didn't see Nicky any more. Like they never see me and Yvonne.

Nicky must've felt rotten about that but we bet she felt even worse about Luke not talking to her. They were such mates before . . . well, who knows, but it must have been an epic barney for him to keep his distance for so long. He just glares out at her from the Sixth Form Common Room, arms folded, mouth down, and I'm glad it's neither of us on the end of his poison looks! I said to Yvonne I could feel his daggers in my back when I made her come with me to ask Nicky how her mum was doing and would it be OK to pop in and see her with a Christmas card. Then Yvonne wanted to know what was playing in Nicky's cans and I asked if her book was any good. Next thing we all headed into choir together.

Lisa Marie stopped Nicky in the corridor. Told her she'd landed the same mark as Elaine in her Christmas maths exam.

'I accused Luke of dressing up as you to sit the paper,' Lisa Marie chuckled and shook Nicky's hand. 'Did he say?'

'No, Mr Presley,' Nicky answered, looking nearly as crestfallen as she did when Jacko caught her outside music and proclaimed loud enough for the whole school to hear, 'Nicola Nevin, your piece on the persecution of minorities was better than one of Luke's speeches. I've told him to dragoon you into my debating club. Has he twisted your arm?'

'Not yet, sir,' Nicky said. And there were tears in her eyes this time.

Must have been one of those days, because there were more tears when Yvonne and I went home with her. The pair of us are like that. One sets the other off. And we were that pleased to see Mrs Nevin again after so long. We'd really missed her.

She said she'd missed us too. Gave us the biggest hug. Told us the last visitor was Lizzie Brownie two months ago. While Nicky was in the kitchen making tea Mrs Nevin showed us all this bag of oils Lizzie had left behind.

She asked us if we knew what had happened to her. Said she was sure Lizzie was the reason Luke and Nicky weren't talking any more. Mrs Nevin said she was worried sick.

'Nicola says nothing and Luke just says what's done cannot be undone when I ask whatever's going on between them. He'll only stay in the same room as Nicola when she's rubbing my hands and feet with the oils. Then he stares at us both like he's hypnotised. You're sure you don't know what happened?'

When I shook my head Mrs Nevin shrugged. 'Well, you're both here now,' she smiled. Told us Luke had ordered Nicky a book about massage for Christmas.

Yvonne and I both said the same thing when we heard that:

'It's a start.'

42

LIZZIE

SUN SIGN: PISCES ♓

RULING PLANET: JUPITER ♃

Conflicting Sun signs: Leo and Scorpio

Pisceans are interested in all things psychic and mystical.

Many claim to have a sixth sense.

Typically they exude an air of mystery.

They never like others to know too much about them . . .

Granny was right.

Best flit before trouble starts. Soon as there's folk agin you. No point in the likes of us waiting to see what others have in store. They'll hardly crown you Queen of the May!

Nearly left it too late. Heart ruling the head. Never supposed to do that. I was well warned. In my cards. In my leaves. In my water. By that scratch that went nowhere deep enough to bleed me powerless . . .

It's just that I never knew I could feel so much for a

boy till I met Luke Nevin.

'Cabbage for brains!' Granny would have been at me if I'd told her about *Nicky* Nevin. Her name alone should have been enough to put me on guard, never mind the way she looked at me.

But how could I ever think a girl like *Nicky* had the power to persuade anyone to do anything? Her witch's name was coincidence: *nicnevin*. She was her brother's sister, and her mother's daughter. They'd decentness shining out like sunshine. That had to count for something. And I didn't fear Nicky either. I pitied her, poor wee stray after scraps. She was so *hungry* it made me cringe, the way she'd laugh at Isabella's bitching and catcalling, far too long and far too loud. Then the others'd rip the piss out her for doing it. And she'd just stand there and take it, glaiket grin on her no matter what Isabella said. With those train tracks biting into her teeth, that smile was more like a grimace of pain.

How could anyone weak as that hurt me?

'Give up, hen,' I felt like whispering to her sometimes. 'You'll never fit in.' Could have put my arm round her. I didn't use my foresight to figure her situation because I didn't need to. That's why I let myself get closer to Nicky

Nevin than was safe. She always looked so *crushed*. Except when she sang. Then her voice was sweet, and I told her so. *Praise where praise is due works better than any charm,* Granny taught me. Singing was one wee thing we had in common, and with Nicky being such an outsider I thought she could do with a compliment.

There was one of my mistakes: ignoring how desperate Nicky was to belong. Didn't consider how far she'd go . . . Well, I blame my healer's instincts. Was trying to help her same as I helped her mum. *Should always be more careful,* Granny would have warned me. *What's your sixth sense for, girlie? Foretelling bad weather?*

Oh Granny!

If you'd still been alive the day I went to that pond and that park, it wouldn't have mattered what Nicky Nevin wished on me. I'd've shot the crow. Before Luke worked the double whammy and paralysed my wit when he smiled his big smile at me, me, *me,* I'd've been gone. Safe. And my disappearance would've have had nothing to do with the boils and itching I cast.

Mind, I'd've had the tongue-lashing of my life for that if Granny had known how I paid back the teasing I took.

No malefice unless your life's on the line, girlie. You tell me your worries first. Then we decide what's best for you.

Of course, Granny or no Granny I should've run off soon as I found the ring of ground behind that pool people mistake for the Drowning Pond in Merlock Park. What a place that is! The whole park's full of bad, but it doesn't touch the darkness of that *real* Drowning Pond up there! I felt myself drawn to it though I didn't want to be and when I walked over it, this chill ran through the core of me though the sun was beating down. All my bones ached like they'd been twisted and crushed and beaten, and I felt the soil sucking at my feet. There were cries and curses echoing round the trees, women's voices pleading for their lives. Covering my ears only made the voices louder. And nobody heard but me.

I should never have hung around. That one visit to Merlock was enough. And I was daft to return on Hallowe'en with that lot! But I couldn't help myself by then. I'd spent a whole year floundering, wondering if there'd ever be anyone to patch even a piece of the hole Granny had torn in my heart when she died. And don't get me wrong, most of my house mothers meant well. Really well. They were good and kind, but the nitty gritty of life meant I was just passing through with all of them. It didn't do to grow close when a relationship was officially temporary. So everyone I met kept their distance.

Till . . .

Well, as the slogan for the adoption campaign goes, I was Tired Of Being Alone. So tired I dropped my guard even though I sensed danger. I let Luke Nevin's affection flood my head till I couldn't think straight. Ended up convincing myself his sister's gossip wouldn't harm me.

Oh my daft girlie, Granny would have said.

The only way the likes of you and me survive this life is swimming hard to stay afloat.